FLAMES
— IN —
AMBER

Cautionary Tales
of Action and Inaction

Crimson Publishing

Jiayi Luo

Flames in Amber: Cautionary Tales of Action and Inaction

DESIGN: Christa Mella

Crimson Publishing
Tucson, AZ

ISBN : 978-1-7341680-1-3

To Lian and Xiaohua.

TABLE OF CONTENTS

Action

MIRRORED

It was one of my recurring dreams, one set in a dizzying labyrinth of mirrors.

Ceiling, floor, walls, you name it—every surface in the narrow passages was endless, reflective silver. In these, I saw not just my own reflection, but also the haggard specter of my father. His image multiplied, empty and eternal, as the mirrors reflected each other.

It was like this in my waking life, too. There was not a living soul who did not know of my father, of his art. If Leonardo da Vinci was the greatest creator in the world before the modern age, then my father was surely the greatest of our time.

Unnerved, I turned, only to see countless fathers turning toward *me* with wandering eyes. Eventually, he stopped echoing my movements and hurried off on his own, marching forward while I trailed behind, weak in every limb, terrified. Abruptly, around the next bend, he opened one of the mirror panels wide: a hidden door.

Briefly, daffodil-colored light limned his age-freckled countenance. He glanced over his shoulder at me, his weary eyes unreadable, before vanishing into whatever lay beyond.

My father left me alone in the labyrinth without a trace of any lingering reflection, not even my own. Emptiness weighed in on me, inescapable, a crushing sense of *loss*—

I woke up, gasping, under the canopy of my father's *Acacia Tree,* of which he'd fashioned the trunk from welded-bronze poles and black-painted barbed wire. Mirror shards were suspended from its abstract, crooked branches—reflective sides down. This sculpture had been in such high demand in the years following its completion that he had worked with a handful of the world's most prestigious museums—New York's MoMA, Boston's MFA, London's Tate Modern, Tokyo's MCA, Beijing's Palace Museum—to install outdoor replicas.

The sky overhead was flawless, stainless blue. The crushing sensation on my chest was my intertwined hands, but I didn't lift them just yet. An itch of pain circled at the back of my mind, an eel chasing its own tail. This was how the dream tended to linger.

I squinted, peering into the mirror fragments overhead. Unsettlingly, my father was still there. Although fractured by the pieces' swaying in the autumn breeze, his features were discernible. His thin lips were fractionally parted, reflected in one fragment. His unpierced ear glimmered in another. One of his wary, narrowed eyes in yet another, illuminated in restless amber as it caught the falling sun—

I was fiercely, inexplicably relieved.

For nearly the past five years, I'd been seeing my father's image instead of my own in every mirror I passed. If he were to vanish, like in my dreams, what would fill the void in his absence? I could never brood on the question for long, although billboards, online advertisements, and even T-shirts that passed me in the street would remind me afresh.

I stood up, dusting dry, fragile leaf slivers from my coat. A minimalist publicity poster on one ivy-covered wall of the ranch house read *Yankai Bai: Retrospective 1974-1989,* annotated near the bottom with an explanation that this exhibition had been installed, here, in the house my father had occupied for the last six years of his life. Unprecedented crowds were expected, to the point that perhaps the installation would become permanent, enshrining his old home.

As the artist's only child, I was permitted solitary entry the day before the exhibition was set to open. I imagined how, the next day, this very front yard would be full of visitors—not just

8

the friends my father had made during his decade-long residence in New York City, but colleagues and admirers from nearly every continent in the world.

Father had often told me that I was excruciatingly shy during our New York days, that I was *infamous*—his word, not mine—for not accepting sweets from his colleagues. Instead, I would just stare at them with intense black eyes, my cheeks rigid in spite of the baby fat I hadn't yet shed. I'd smile wryly every time he related this particular anecdote.

For me, New York had been a dull, numbing blur punctuated by only a few points of daffodil-colored light. My chronological memories began with our first unbearably silent night in the city, and continued with the pale blue curves of morning emerging from beneath the curtains. I once asked him why we'd moved away from *the noisy high places*—by which I meant the various tiny workshops we'd once occupied in Lower Manhattan—to this quiet, lowly ranch house.

My father said the city's crowds had terrified me, turned me into a girl devoid of smiles. "I want my Ai to feel safe and comfortable, to grow up healthy," he said. So I smiled, felt safer and more comfortable after internalizing his reassurances.

After all, *everyone* smiled at him, even people who had never met him.

I latched the gate behind me as I left the ranch house yard, and it closed with a rusty shriek. I made my way up the front walk and pushed open the door of my father's memory-ridden house.

The interior was bathed in dim light. Sculptures seemed to writhe in the low light. Gelatin silver photographs and oil paintings, both framed and unframed, hung on the walls and adorned strategically placed wooden easels. It was Mr. Lončar, the current owner of the ranch house and one of my father's closest friends, who had suggested renovating the house to transform it into a gallery for my father's retrospective. The result was stunning, as all of my father's pieces looked just the way they were meant to—as enigmatic as my father had looked in life.

Once, I had considered my father no different from any other high-school art teacher. He was the bland, average kind that walked the art room's periphery as his students worked. He'd scrutinize their projects from various angles, intermittently offering laconic advice. If the older girls in his class stared with strange light in their eyes, and their parents glanced away when they saw him, it was because he didn't look like them.

Of course, in exactly the same fashion, I didn't look like any of the other kids in my elementary school. Stacie Fulton, the younger sister of one of his students, cornered me with her friends in tow and taunted me with claims that my father was an *avant-gardist*. Abashedly, I had to ask them what it meant, as the term had an unfamiliar ring to it.

"Are you stupid?" Stacie glared at me. "It means he makes his students doodle weird stuff," she continued, glaring some more. "Lines and circles, what they truly *feel*, or whatever. The school doesn't pay him to teach that kind of crap. It's such a shame. For an international superstar, your dad's nothing but a useless yellow punk."

That day, I went home with ten aching fingers and livid scratches on my wrists. Father was sitting at our dining table with the telephone receiver in one hand and a hand mirror in the other. He asked me what I had done at school that day, but his eyes were still fixed on the mirror.

"Got into a fight with a classmate," I said dully.

My father raised his head. Heavily, he sighed.

"You almost strangled that girl to death, Ai."

The leadenness of his statement strangled *me*. Excuses crowded in my chest: *I didn't mean to—it didn't even feel real—you would have backed me up if you'd been there!* My faith shattered like so much glass, cascading down the raw interior of my rib cage.

Father did not ask why I'd done it. Instead, he turned back to the hand mirror with a wistful, bitter curve to his lips. He smashed the mirror on the freshly waxed floor.

Lingering in front of a painting called *Dance*, I was keenly aware that it hung right next to where he'd shattered the mirror all those years ago. I recalled how my father, frowning into the jagged slivers at his feet, had been stiffly seated at the now-absent table.

"Violent," he lamented, shaking his head. "You are always this way, Ai."

Dance—an austere strip of black-saturated canvas upon which expressively irregular dashes of beige, grey, and white intermingled—was preserved in a narrow wooden frame fitted with a pane of conservation glass. As lamplight from overhead bathed its textured surface, I spotted my father's face in the void of its backdrop. He peered through the pale web of dashes.

I peered back, an unexpected surge of sentimentality weighing on my chest.

Father, the notorious loner, the renowned enigma, the much-sainted exile—whose past I didn't share, whose motivations I couldn't guess. Father, whose lips froze in a fleeting moment of remembrance between toasts, aching against a backdrop of hilarity and banter in the metropolitan night. Father, who had grown solemn—despondent, even—ever since I assaulted the younger Fulton girl and he smashed that hand mirror. Father, who left post-shower fog on the bathroom mirror undisturbed, who instead preferred to shave in his ill-lit bedroom. Father, who covered the full-length mirror in that same room with the curtain from his only window.

Father, who lit cigarettes in the backyard without taking a puff, coatless in the winter dusk, unaware I had called out to him as I returned home—lonely in spite of his fame.

My father's distant, perpetual melancholy was the reason I put on a smile as we walked into the coffee shop where Emil Hono, one of father's students, worked part-time during his college freshman year. I could see why my father loved him. Sometimes, I thought I might've fallen for him myself, had I been in my father's shoes.

Emil was the image of cherubic glamor. He frequently had to flash his student ID in order to convince customers he was an adult. Perhaps without benefit of proof, those perplexed patrons wouldn't have been able to imagine how Emil behaved in intimate settings. Every flash of his slim fingers, every glance from his shadowed eyes, reeked of Rrose Sélavy—or the scent-personification some other artist's pseudonym, the conceptual opposite of innocence.

The fact that Emil's sophistication enthralled my father was a source of misery for me, especially when Emil moved into our ranch house. My father insisted that it was the kind thing to do, given his wealth and influence. He could both provide for Emil's day-to-day needs and also see to it that the young man received the finest education available.

I felt suffocating inferiority when Emil spoke kindly to me. The delight my father took in his presence had once belonged to *me*.

There had been so much going on at the same time—suspicious glances and loud muttering from our neighbors, from his students, and from my schoolmates. Curse words, deeply carved, appeared on my desk at the back corner of the classroom. The only secondary school I could attend in the area was Catholic, which resulted in the skirmish with Stacie Fulton.

Some anonymous menace wrote, in permanent marker on the back cover of my study Bible, *YELLOW FAGS GO TO HELL.* I wrapped the book in oilskin, under the pretense of protecting its precious leather binding, and was commended by the Sister who taught my religion class.

At home, I endured an ominous, persistent racket from the attic every night as I lay in bed.

I distracted myself by remembering all of the times my father had fondly complimented me. When I found an exquisite conch shell as we roamed the beach; when I accepted a lollipop from Mr. Lončar for the first time; when I doodled shapelessly on drafting paper, imitating his style, and he sneaked it into one of his exhibitions; when he gazed down at me as he led me through the bustling streets of Manhattan, squeezing my hand with a smile.

One night, I snuck up the stairs and peered through the half-open attic door. There was father, seated in a dining chair with his back facing the door, his gaze drifting between the center of the room and the far wall, on which a long, black-painted rectangle of canvas was hung.

And there was Emil—dancing wildly, gracefully uncontrolled—in the middle of the floor. He wore a gauzy, iridescent white cocktail dress. The movements of his pale arms possessed an uncanny grace—like moon-colored eels, circling, chasing their own tails. He pivoted, appearing to stagger for a moment in his elegant heeled ankle boots. His eyes were closed, the lids painted austere black against the backdrop of his pearly, powdered features.

Father's reflection in *Dance*, trapped behind the webbing of Emil's haphazard vines, sighed as I sighed. Father had painted many other shapes on Emil's face: severe squares, meandering calligraphy, the outline of a goat's skull, Yayoi Kusama's iconic *Pumpkin*, and the word *APOLLO* with a Greek Δ in place of *A*. These arcane symbols formed my father's famous sequence of lithographs, *Répliques Vivantes*, which now hung neatly in the longest corridor connecting the ranch house's former living room and garage. These, too, had been replicated for international consumption, and the revenue from commercial reproductions was vast.

The brushstrokes on Emil's face and bare shoulders, as well as Emil's dispassionate expression, reminded me of how I yearned, at that time, for my father to paint *me*.

This covert longing for black pigment on my skin came to a jarring end the day I woke up after falling asleep in religion class. I opened my eyes to see Stacie Fulton and her friends—exactly the same pack as on the day I almost strangled her—surrounding me and chuckling.

One of them gave me a hand mirror. In its unyielding, silvery surface, I could see a sentence written across my face. I was unable to read the letters' reversed reflection.

"Need me to read it for you?" Stacie sneered. "It says 'daughter of a homosexual pedophile.' What do you think of that?"

Her friends twittered derisively, a hurtful, cacophonous chorus: *All capitalized—in permanent marker—looks great on you, Ai, really!*

"Who taught you the words 'homosexual pedophile'?" I asked.

"Dumb question," Stacie shot back. "My father did, of course."

"Did he teach you 'yellow fags go to hell' as well?" I retorted.

"What?" Stacie asked, wide-eyed, feigning vacant innocence.

Wrong. It was *all* wrong. So much wrongness everywhere.

I glanced surreptitiously at the front of the classroom. Sister was not looking, had likely *never* been looking. I grabbed Stacie by the collar, yanking her down.

That day, I limped all the way home with a black eye and grazed knuckles, filled to the brim with hate. The idea that some of Stacie's blood remained on my aching joints, mingling with my plasma, nauseated me.

Emil sprang up from his cozy spot on the sofa as I laboriously shoved open the front door. He scarcely had time to blurt *Hey, what happened?* before I picked up the simpering porcelain angel statuette from my father's bookshelf and threw it at him.

The statuette shattered, scattering jagged white shards at Emil's bare feet.

"Get out of here," I said calmly, tear-choked, "and don't ever come back."

Emil stood wide-eyed amidst the porcelain shards. Blood poured from beneath the palm he'd pressed to his forehead, which I'd struck with precision, staining the carpet.

When my father got home from his interrupted teachers' conference, he found me wet faced and curled up in the corner of the bathroom. Emil was nowhere to be seen.

Quietly, my father sat down beside me. He cleaned my grazed knuckles with iodine and scrubbed the demeaning sentence from my face with rubbing alcohol.

In the weeks following, my father called Emil daily, but received no answer. After several months, it was clear that my outburst at Emil had driven him from our home for good. I debated with myself incessantly as to whether I should tell my father, but I never found the nerve. My father's devotion, his full attention, had shifted back to me.

That was also when I realized the depths of his pain, how deeply it was engraved in me.

The retrospective in the ranch house had been arranged in chronological order, rather than by genre or style. His work was so iconic, in every medium he had ever decided to try, that it would all have been instantly recognizable regardless of how it had been organized. Works displayed closest to the front door dated to the end of his career and were largely expressionist in nature. Works displayed closest to the exit were influenced by traditional styles from China, which he had mastered before fleeing into exile.

I wandered between these extremities, experiencing an illusion of time travel along the axis of his life. My reverie was shattered by someone calling my name from the vicinity of *Dance*.

Father regularly sent me postcards and letters after I had transferred to a friendlier boarding high school in the next state over. He told me that he missed me terribly, and that he had started working on a piece that would interest me. After all, I was his Ai, his dearly beloved.

I never answered his correspondence, telling myself it was no less than he deserved. He would never be done paying for the negligence his fame had resulted in, for the attention he had paid to Emil at the expense of being a more attentive father to *me*.

While away at school, I began to research the history of my native country. I envisioned the image of a young, single father between paragraphs describing the relevant generation.

Our seeming mutual tranquility persisted until a chilly morning toward the end of 1989, when father drowned himself on the very beach where I'd once found that conch. While critics and would-be biographers, lining up for miles, called the site of his suicide *poetic* and *rife with meaning*, hell-bent on analyzing his final message. To me, it was obvious. *My* negligence, my failure to respond, had led him there.

I took the news somberly, with the realization that something I could not name was forever lost—as unrecoverable as my father's life. Later that day, when I finally got up and walked past the full-length mirror in my room, I glimpsed a figure both familiar and strange.

Here, in the present, I followed the sound of the voice calling my name.

"It's been a long time, Ai," greeted Emil, with the same veiled smile and kind voice as years ago. "Nice dress, by the way. I like it. Very nostalgic."

Guiltily, I glanced down at the gauzy white cocktail dress I wore beneath my coat. I had adorned its surface with iridescent cellophane cut into the shape of fish scales.

"Father understood the art of copies and replicas," I said tersely. "New meanings, new contexts. I recreated this dress in hopes it might add meaning to the original."

Emil nodded, staring at it, lost in thought. "It kind of does, I guess."

When my father tended to the bruise beneath my eye seven years ago, I'd asked him how we could even go on existing. He'd only sighed, half-turning to face the mirror.

"My father," Emil said, still in contemplation, "was a military man. He was one of those heroes who'd been decorated with a dozen medals, you know? His power was rooted in hyper-masculinity and violence. I've never really figured out how to exist as his son."

Until now, I had never understood why my father glared at his own reflection. He had done so until the very day his image replaced mine in the wake of his passing.

"Your father left a piece of work just for you," Emil said, leading me to my father's bedroom. He unlocked the door with a key of which I'd never had a copy.

I followed Emil inside. My father's full-length mirror stood alone at the center of the empty room, covered with the same heavy curtain from his lone window.

Slowly, I uncovered the mirror to reveal its silvery surface. I expected to see my father's image, instead of my own, wearing a dress adorned with iridescent fish scales.

What I saw instead was webbing formed of brushstrokes. Pale blue paint thinned with turpentine meandered across the mirror, beneath which I saw only myself in the dress.

"Your father named this piece *Ai*," said Emil's reflection, just over my shoulder.

QUIET SPACES

The book, as it was left to Mathilde, was not much to look at. Not all books were visually pleasing, or even needed to be, but the circumstances of this book's existence seemed so uncharacteristic as to constitute a mystery. She always had liked a good puzzle.

The outer leaves were rough, crackled sheets of parchment that seemed to have no sense of what it was they held. Upon her father's death, his library had passed to Mathilde, and the holdings were substantial. Still, it was curious that her father would have commissioned such a plain thing. She had found it tucked in between two lovingly illustrated Latin missals, which she had also looked at, but couldn't read. Mathilde's mother had tried to teach her, but she had always been more interested in sketching ink-splotched cartoons on scrap parchment.

The plain little book, at least, was in English. If it had been French or German or Latin, Mathilde would not have been able to make out even a few words here and there. She could not read any language but the one of her birth, but she could write her name painstakingly with a quill she had trimmed herself. She knew only one style of book-hand, and wrote it badly.

It had been disappointing to discover that the first story in this curious volume was a religious one. At the same time, it could have been worse, because there was a sort of wistful, comforting charm to a father dreaming of his lost daughter's soul in a better place.

By the end of the story, Mathilde hadn't been thinking about the End of the World, or staying pure in order to become the Lord Jesu's bride, or having such thoughts as she should have been having. She was thinking of her father ten days in his grave, wondering what Christ did with good men after they died. She wiped her tears away before they could smudge the ink.

In her father's household, there hadn't been many storytellers.

There had been Mathilde's nurse, who had told her about the Blessed Virgin and the birth of Her Son, and there had been her father's clerk, who, on the back of the household shopping lists, had jotted down little pieces of poetry about brave knights and martyrs and dragons.

Those, Mathilde had always liked to rescue from the rubbish he left in sacks outside his chamber door. She had kept them tucked between her shifts in the chest at the foot of her bed, though her younger sisters more often than not got at them and asked her what they said.

If the poems tilted scandalous, which they more often than not did, Mathilde made up alternative lines as she went along. Both Mathilde's sisters and the servants' daughters seemed to know they were getting the short shrift, none of the juicy stuff, and got bored fast.

There had been Father John, who had been to Mathilde more like an uncle than a priest. His tales were her favorite, but they had spilled from his mouth as easily as the Mass, and she couldn't think that he would have been allowed to write them as he'd written Latin books. He was as dead as Mathilde's father, and had been since her fifteenth birthday, which had fallen in the Year of Our Lord thirteen hundred and eighty-one. Two years later, she was married.

Mathilde's husband, Robert, was a kind man—and several years her senior. He had not laughed at her whimsy as so many suitors before him had done. That was kindness enough.

The second and third tales in the curious, fragile book had been worse disappointments than the first. They were her nurse's Bible stories all over again, only in fancier language.

Mathilde read some lines aloud to herself, carefully under her breath, and decided that even if silly Jonah had sort of deserved what he got between Nineveh and the whale, well—whoever had written his tale down in the Holy Book could at least have put it in poetry like Solomon had set his songs. They hadn't had her language in those days, though, and she understood that translating God's Word from the Hebrew into Latin was not heresy like translating it into English. There were folks in London trying to change that.

Mathilde read through to the end, so engrossed that she lost track of the time. If the story-poems preceding this long one, the longest of all, had been enjoyable, then she didn't have sufficient words for how she felt about the grand finale.

Now, on the book's last page, in the quiet space at the end, her hand was shaking.

The Latin motto at the end probably had nothing to do with anything. In tales of romance, it rarely did. Mathilde traced the last stroke of the pen with her index finger, trying to remember the clerk's handwriting. This was a story like he would have tried to tell, only it was much, much longer, and it was as exciting as the French books her mother used to read and then tell her as she and her sisters sat stitching in the evenings.

Mathilde knew about King Arthur. She was convinced that anybody who didn't had been living at the bottom of a moat for their entire lives and had probably been born down there, too.

She knew about the sad, beautiful Guinevere, and she knew about handsome, noble Lancelot. She knew about Gawain, too, though the stories her mother had told her about him were nothing like the story she had just read. Her mother had never mentioned a Green Knight or a green horse or a dark, forbidding castle right in the middle of the woods where her father had gone hunting almost every day. Her husband liked to hunt there almost as often.

Carefully, Mathilde wrapped the little book in her sleeve and clutched it to her chest.

There had been no pictures to show what was contained in the wild, winding words. No lovingly painted river with gemstones and fish, no trees and spices in the garden, no terrifying storms and betrayals at sea, and no bloody axe and astonished faces.

The stairs were damp with remnants of recent rain, but Mathilde could find her way down them in the dark, leaving her husband's library far behind. She wasn't going to bother with her cloak, because the night was bound to be thick with mist.

The door was barred, but it was easy enough to lift. Whoever said that carrying a baby was hard enough work had been mistaken; Mathilde was as strong as an ox, with her heavy, round belly and a book clutched over her heart.

The courtyard was muddy, and Mathilde's shoes sank and scraped in the mud. Her skirts almost tripped her, but her husband had stopped chiding her for her ruined hems. He was a rich man, and he could not be bothered to refuse something as simple as stitching repairs or new gowns altogether. Mathilde's life had been easy in comparison to her mother's.

From where Mathilde stood, the sky overhead looked like black soot sprinkled with tiny white diamonds. She wondered if the writer of the book would have thought that. She wondered if it was what Sir Gawain had seen when he left Arthur's courtyard with his shield drawn up tight under his chin and a troubled look in his clear eyes. He had faced not rain, but ice.

Mathilde rushed past the gate and into the road, gasping suddenly for breath. The mist was as thick as she had imagined it, and far down the thoroughfare, past the village and over the hills, the wood appeared as a sea of dark and starless leaves in the night.

Chilled, she wrapped the book more tightly in her sleeve to keep it from getting damp.

What Mathilde wanted to do was take her mare (no Gryngolet, her Bellefleur, but a serviceable steed nonetheless) and fly down the winding road into the dark. The Green Knight's castle seemed a friendly place, full of warm wonders that her husband would have had a hard time getting his head around. With a resigned sigh, she turned and retraced her steps.

In the morning, Mathilde's husband shook her awake in her library chair and asked why she had tracked mud all over their floor. She told him that it was too hot in there at night, and she had just needed to get some air for his strapping son. Her husband could not argue with this, and set a hand on her stomach, proclaiming that he could feel the lad growing sure enough.

Later that night, once more in the library, Mathilde approached her husband's desk and set her hands on his shoulders. She ran her fingers through his wind-tangled hair and asked him if the hunt had been good. He responded with an idle noise and turned the page of his psalter.

Mathilde tickled behind Robert's wind-burnt ears, and he jumped.

"My lord," she said, running one finger from his earlobe down to the other ticklish spot just beneath his collar. "I would like to ask you a favor."

Robert fidgeted in his seat, smiling fondly at her.

"I will order your new gown tomorrow."

"I don't want a new gown. I wasn't fond of that one anyway."

Robert sighed heavily, eyeing Mathilde's expanding middle.

"You'll need one to replace it. My son is getting bigger."

"I want to make a book," Mathilde said, working both hands into his tunic now, stretching the linen enough to get both hands underneath, "for your son."

"A book? What manner of book?" Robert asked, clearly intrigued.

"A book with stories and pictures such as a bright boy ought to be taught to read from," Mathilde said, murmuring in his ear. "It will have the story of Jonah and the great whale, and it will have the story of Sir Gawain, who was an honorable knight."

Her kind, indulgent husband didn't seem to be listening, which was mostly her intent.

"I will...ask Father Wilhelm if...he can make such a book."

"No," Mathilde corrected him, withdrawing her hands. "You will order many blank vellum sheets from the abbey, and have them delivered unbound."

Robert chuckled. "You cannot read to my son from a blank book."

"Of course I cannot," Mathilde said, pinching his side. "I will need inks and quills in order to copy the stories from an old book I found. I will need fine paints for the pictures."

Her husband snorted, half strained laughter and half a long-suffering groan.

"I will not be able to get fine paints. Colored inks, perhaps, but costly pigments for my frivolous wife to make nonsense on blank pages?"

"I don't care," Mathilde said, poking his stomach. "Your son will have a book."

Her husband remained quiet for a moment, trying to control his ticklish breath.

"A book copied and drawn in his mother's own hand."

"Yes, why should he not have such a rare gift?"

Her husband laughed, grabbed her hand, and kissed it. "They told me that you would make a selfish wife."

"I am selfish," Mathilde agreed. "I took you for myself."

Much later, by the cold moonlight that lit her chamber and fell on her husband's face, Mathilde thought about the little book hidden in the linen chest at the foot of her bed. She told the stories over again to herself, imagining the way that she would draw them. The old book had empty spaces, but there was not enough room in them.

Mathilde had always thought that shoving pictures into tiny squares and into cramped margins was the product of men's stupidity. Pictures needed whole pages to themselves, and they needed to have lots of action and maybe a little bit of blood.

The words, she would copy, but the pictures, she would make fresh and new as Eden. She would instruct Baerd, their steward, to obtain the pigments at his earliest convenience, and she would slate her oldest gown—the one with the newly muddy hem—for working in.

Satisfied with her plans to make a gift for her unborn son, Mathilde slept soundly.

In the days that followed, Mathilde took loose, blank flyleaves from the older tomes in the library, resolved to practice what she had not done in several years. Her childhood sketches had been admirable, at least according to Father John—creatures more recognizable and lively than any apprentice scribe he'd yet seen. Mathilde had even considered joining a nunnery, so as to spend her life in a scriptorium doing what, at the time, she loved best.

Just shy of a decade after she'd formed those aspirations, Robert changed the course of her life. She had asked him, on their wedding day, if she might train with the sisters in the convent at Amesbury. He had chuckled and said, What noble lady wants ink-stained fingers?

This lady, Mathilde thought in response to the memory, dipping her quill in some plain brown iron-gall ink. She thought about what she might draw, about what she had once drawn to her mother's frustration and her sisters' amusement. There had been cats living in the stables, and litters of kittens come spring. She'd once drawn the lot with human faces, which had given one of her sisters nightmares for a week. She wasn't allowed to draw monstrosities after that.

The monstrosity emerging on Mathilde's present-day page was monstrous for a different reason—the likeness of her spirited mare, Bellefleur, was exact. Even through several years without practice, she had retained something of the uncanny talent of her youth.

Mathilde added the smallest details she could think of, worked on the drawing for hours. In the absence of other pigments, she couldn't add color. Still, the drawing engrossed her.

When the household steward's wife saw it the next day on one of her rare visits inside the manor house, she asked Mathilde who had done it. Proudly, Mathilde told her.

The steward's wife offered her a reasonable sum for the piece, so she sold it.

With Robert away for the next week to visit his aging mother and unmarried younger brother in the outskirts of London, there was not much for Mathilde to do in her present condition. By the time he returned, she had filled several blank sheets with detailed roadside flowers and late-harvest apples from local market stalls, as well as the women who ran them.

The steward's wife must have been at her usual gossip, because the wives from two neighboring manor houses had come to look at Mathilde's drawings. Several sold.

"You're getting good," Robert said encouragingly, if blandly. "I've brought you some pigments. Are you sure there's time enough for what your project demands? You'll be laid up for a spell when the babe arrives, and busy supervising the wet nurse once you're well."

Heavier with child than ever, Mathilde wobbled to her feet and kissed his cheek.

"I'm not as fragile as all that! I'll be on my feet and riding again soon enough."

The midwife's reassurances said that she had some weeks left to go, perhaps a month or more, before the baby's arrival. That was time enough to practice, time enough to perfect mixing the set of colored mineral powders with precious acacia gum and water.

The wet nurse's young son, Daniel, came to the library to watch her work. His mother, too, would soon give birth, and Daniel's interest in both infants she'd be caring for was keen.

"Cows are not usually that color," he pointed out, elbows resting heavily on the desk.

"That's because it's not a cow," Mathilde said, faintly piqued. "It's my favorite horse."

"Bellefleur is not that color," Daniel giggled, running his finger through a smudge of ink.

"A roan shade like that is difficult to mix," Mathilde replied. "I'd like to see you try."

By dusk, all that they had in doing was making messes of their hands and clothes, and the full-color piece of Bellefleur with Daniel feeding her an apple went home with the boy, to his mother. Mathilde expected no compensation, saying his mother's service was enough.

That night, the wet nurse went into labor, and Daniel rushed to Mathilde in the stables the next morning to tell her the birth had produced not one child, but twins.

"Mam will be unwell too long," he said, "and she will need to care for my sisters."

"I suppose that's her way of saying two's fine to nurse, but three's drawing a line?"

"Yes, Lady," Daniel said, apologetically twisting a strand of his long hair, and left.

Mathilde thought about her prospects of finding another wet nurse in their village on such short notice and decided it was worth neither the bother, nor the coin. That settled the matter. She would nurse her son—she hoped for a son, so as to make Robert proud—herself.

Robert was not pleased to hear of the additional strain on her, although he supposed the funds saved would permit them finer christening festivities. He told Baerd to acquire extra wine.

Sleepless with her condition, Mathilde pored over the little book by night, running her fingers over the spaces she longed to fill. By day, she mixed colors, trial and error, obsessed with getting each shade right. When she was young, Father John had mixed them for her.

In the days to follow, more locals—some tradesmen now, not just their wives, as well as a lord from one of the neighboring manors—called on her for commissions. Word of her swift, precise work had spread. Most wanted pictures of loved ones, and gave detailed descriptions, which Mathilde noted down and worked from.

Still others wanted matter more fantastical—strange images from their dreams, religious fervor intermingled with the whimsical, even the sensual. Mathilde saw no harm in producing these images for private consumption. They brought people joy.

Robert did not seem to begrudge her the attention. He did not take the time to do more than glance at her work, either. He suggested she use the funds to find a new nurse, as surely his son would arrive soon. He thanked God she had at least found distraction.

Several weeks passed, with more and more of Mathilde's art trickling into the world, with the book for her child still unaltered—and then, Mathilde went into labor.

She had never known such pain, and she had survived the plague in her youth. Hours stretched into a day. She slipped in and out of waking fever-dreams, horrors and fancies she'd drawn for others, from whatever pain-easing drink her maidservant continually administered.

A day and a night and half another day was how long it took Mathilde's son to come.

When Mathilde woke from exhausted slumber, Robert was at her side. He held the child.

"We should set the christening a week hence," he said, stroking Mathilde's damp hair. "All who wish to attend may come from the chapel after Mass, for drink and celebration."

Mathilde only nodded, reaching to weakly stroke the baby's foot. "That will work."

"We must think of a name," Robert said, "and you must finish the picture-book."

Mathilde closed her eyes. "I have some commissions to finish," she replied.

"Well, finish them while you're laid up," Robert said, "and find a nurse."

The three pieces left in her queue were more complex, images that might have been more at home in fever-dream altarpieces those madmen in the Low Countries seemed to paint. Demons and angels and mortals all intermingled; animals personified like the human-faced cats Mathilde had painted when she was younger.

She worked on them in between bouts of nursing and calming Audric, consulting her patrons' descriptions. Her reputation for precise anatomy, it seemed, had taken the foreground. Well, if those Dutch eccentrics could paint debauchery, so could she.

Within a month of the last several pieces being completed and sent to their patrons, word reached Robert that Church authorities had been sent throughout the surrounding villages to investigate heretical iconography. He begged her to take no further commissions, lest she be mistaken for the source.

But I am the source, Mathilde thought, holding Audric tighter. Since when are the imaginings of a mere woman heretical, what when men in far-off lands produce worse?

It took only another month—less, perhaps, by precise calendar reckoning—for one of Mathilde's patrons to reveal her as the source. The Church sent authorities to the manor, with whom Robert spent several hours talking in the library, which was also Mathilde's workshop. Mathilde listened at the door, with Audric asleep on her shoulder, but could make out little of the proceedings.

Robert emerged before Mathilde could creep off again. He took Audric from her arms before she could protest, angry and pained, followed closely by the stern men in vestments. The priests seemed to be waiting on Robert, as if it fell to him to speak.

"I must ask you to go," Robert said haltingly, "and take your heresy with you."

"This makes little sense," Mathilde pleaded in disbelief. "I made what others wished. I do not put stock in the things I painted. The heresy lies with them!"

"They shall be dealt with justly," sniffed one of the priests, "at the gallows."

"Then why is my fate not the same?" Mathilde demanded, enraged. "Why?"

"Because you were but the instrument," said Robert, "and because I begged."

"Begged them spare my life?" Mathilde asked, heartbroken. "Do they not know being parted from my son is death in its own right?"

"Such suffering will suit your crime," agreed the first priest. "We will work to find the others out, not knowing the precise reach of your...indiscretions. If you would offer up the names not on this list"—he handed her a piece of rolled parchment—"then perhaps we may be swayed to leniency. Send you to a nunnery for several years' penance and labor. Then, perhaps, Lord Robert may take you back."

I will not betray them, Mathilde thought, turning away, even as they've betrayed me.

She would find her way in the world, perhaps, by her vision and skill—the Low Countries might be a start, although she did not know their customs or tongue.

Loss and ruin, Mathilde would leave in her wake. She hoped that some of the accused—some of those strange, quiet spaces she had created—might yet survive.

Action

RANN

My little sister, Rann, grew up with an innate insensitivity to pain.

I realized this for the first time as we were strolling along a brook in the countryside. It was breezy that day. We were both small at the time; she was five, and I was eight. As I led her by the hand, we were lagging behind our father and older sisters.

Eventually, she tripped on a rock and skinned her knees. I felt a jolt of dismay, or at least I *thought* it was dismay. Whatever it was, I was also excited.

Great, I thought, in denial. *Now she'll scream and cry and embarrass the hell out of me.*

At that point in my life, I was terrified at the mere existence of girls. Girls whispering in my family, girls taunting on the school playground. Girls chattering among themselves, girls giggling in lowered voices, girls brazenly playing make-believe. Girls in the street who called out to me and then dismissed me with a disdainful wave. Girls in the sandbox who asked me for help and then shoveled sand down my collar. Girls in the school library who wept just because I happened to borrow the last copy of their favorite graphic novel.

My relationship with my sisters was especially rough, even though I loved them.

Izumi constantly played mother, nagging me to do homework as I neared the climax of a graphic novel. Fuyutsuki was the bully, who dumped the contents of my backpack in search of pocket change.

And Rann, the youngest and dearest to me, was frightening. She either maintained dead silence or burst out screaming, depending on the circumstances. There was no predicting it.

Rann was in high spirits that day beside the stream. I wished with all my heart for her to remain so, until we reached Father's hometown.

When she skinned her knees, I almost clapped my hands over my ears.

But, to my surprise, she didn't make a sound. She just bent to look at her wounds and, without hesitation, peeled away the dead skin that had sloughed off the pink flesh beneath.

"What are you doing?" I asked, in horrified fascination.

I felt horrified because she couldn't feel pain, couldn't know how badly she was hurt. I wanted to take her pain, experience it for her. I thought the notion pleased me because my only desire had ever been to protect her. But the fascination...

"Cleaning," Rann replied matter-of-factly, still picking.

"Doesn't it hurt?" I asked, peering beneath her wild hair.

Rann looked up, blankly staring back at me

"What is hurt?" she asked, uncomprehending.

***

Another time, Rann asked Izumi to teach her how to embroider.

Izumi was working golden chrysanthemums on crimson fabric.

"Really? You want to learn this?" She smiled. "That's a pleasant surprise. You've got to pay attention, though. It'll hurt if you stab your finger."

Izumi demonstrated a few basic stitches for Rann, and then gave her a piece of fabric and some golden floss to play with.

From my spot on the couch next to Rann, behind the pages of a bland British detective novel, I watched vigilantly as Rann clumsily pushed her needle up and down through the pulled-taut fabric. The moment I read a bit more in my book is when it happened.

"Why did the thread turn red?" Rann complained. "I can't see."

No way, I thought. *I only looked away for a few seconds.*

Tossing my book aside, I grabbed her hand and turned the embroidery hoop over.

There it was—she had pricked her middle finger with the needle, pulled the thread clean through her flesh, and continued her attempts to embroider the blood-colored fabric.

For long moments, I felt an undeniable thrill, and couldn't look away.

When I finally took her to clean and bandage her wounds, I felt awful.

***

On another occasion, Rann insisted on helping Fuyutsuki prepare vegetables for dinner.

"Great," Fuyutsuki said. "You just cut the stuff up and pile it so Izumi knows it's ready. Piece of cake. See how I cut that carrot? I'll leave the rest to you."

She left the kitchen, wiped her hands on her pants, turned on the TV, and flopped on the couch. Any excuse to get out of completing a task for Izumi, she would take.

I remember storming out of my room while having an argument with Fuyutsuki. She had turned the volume all the way up while I was practicing the violin in my room.

Father had wanted all of us to take up musical instruments, but I was the only one who tried, let alone followed through. I was intensely annoyed at Fuyutsuki that day.

Too irked to notice Rann's back facing me from the kitchen, I missed the fact that she had just grabbed a huge, unwieldy kitchen knife with her tiny, feeble hand.

Izumi walked into the kitchen half an hour later to find a pile of irregular carrot-cubes drenched in blood. Accustomed to Rann's catastrophes, she rinsed the cubes and added them to the beef-curry stew. At least the curry would cover any remaining trace.

That same summer afternoon, I took Rann to the pharmacy across the street. I watched while the pharmacist disinfected and dressed the cuts on her hands. I couldn't look away.

"You're a brave one," said the pharmacist. "Any other kid your age would be sobbing, but here you are. Sitting still as a stone."

Rann blinked at the old man—then yawned and burped.

"Ha!" The pharmacist was amused. "I guess if you weren't such a tough girl, you wouldn't have ended up hurting yourself to begin with."

There was also the annual handicraft project for her art class. The time she used Father's tools to try and repair her broken radio. Her sudden curiosity about the electric blender.

Rann was always fascinated with something that would inevitably bring her to harm.

"Impressive," Izumi said to me once, "how you handle Rann's calamities with such calm."

"Calm? I doubt it." I washed the last traces of blood off a rag, watching the gorgeous red tendrils disperse in the water. "I only keep steady for Rann's sake."

I didn't mention that I used my feigned implacability to hide part of what I was really feeling. Sorry and hurt on Rann's behalf, yes, but too eager to *experience* what Rann couldn't feel. I had begun to understand; I was too interested even when characters in my graphic and detective novels became seriously injured. I read those scenes over and over.

"No, no," Izumi was quick to respond. "I believe you have the *most* empathy among all of us! You're the one working to protect her tonight, after all."

I wrung out the rag as hard as I could. "Maybe you're right."

"What are you so worried about?" Izumi asked. "You care."

I spread the rag, only to wring it again. Part of me wanted her to guess my secret, so I wouldn't have to be ashamed anymore. I didn't want to have to say it.

"I'm the only one with a separate bedroom, so I can hear everything. *Everything,* Izumi. I can hear Father's footsteps as he approaches your door. I can tell from his steps that he's discovered something else he doesn't want to see. I listen while

34

he drags Rann out of bed and into the living room. I hear every word. He orders Rann to face the wall and take off her shirt. I say *nothing*, lying frozen, while he takes off his belt—"

"Akio," Izumi interrupted, "that's *enough*." She sounded like she was about to cry.

I spread the rag, wrung it, spread it out, and wrung it again. I couldn't look at her.

"Once he's done," I continued, "I can't sleep. Those sounds echo in my head until morning. That's why I fall asleep in class and get a good dressing-down from the teachers."

I wondered if she understood my selfishness, then. What I didn't want to admit.

"Don't talk like that," Izumi said gently, laying her hand on my shoulder. "You don't have to shame yourself by mentioning what happens at school. You don't have to *pretend* to be cold-blooded to save Father's face. I understand. It's the same with me."

"Really?" I glanced toward her in shock, relieved. Maybe she knew Rann was monstrous, too, and was afraid to admit it. Maybe she shared *my* particular malady.

"Yes," she said, tearful, but she was smiling. "It's always good to know you're not alone. Talk to me whenever you need to, okay?"

But do you realize the monstrosity existing side by side with my love? I thought.

"Still, I can't help wondering, why is Rann like this? Does she really not feel?"

"No matter what she's like," I said, gripped by fear at my foolish attempt to make unspoken confession as I hung the rag, "she's our little sister."

To my surprise, Izumi hugged me from behind.

"You're right," she said tearfully. "You're so right!"

It only lasted a moment, but it felt like electrocution.

***

When Father quit his job at the bank, he joined his friend as co-chair of a lumber company.

"Our business is on the rise!" Father waved his cigarette as he spoke to the four of us. "Real-estate rates are booming, so

35

they'll need wood for the luxury properties. High-class people want trees, none of that concrete stuff. No doubt about it."

Gathered around the dining-room table, we all nodded except for Rann.

There were only four seats around the table, and it worked for meals because Father never came home to eat with us. He always ate with clients, colleagues, or the old woman who ran the workingmen's bar across town. Doubtless he talked *her* ear off, too.

But during those late-night lectures he gave us, Rann was always left out. I felt outraged on her behalf, but I also knew that she was too young to hear Father's blustering.

Rann often tried to pull a stool in from the study to sit with us. Once, she even climbed into my lap. Somehow, she regarded me—her protector with a dirty secret—as her closest friend among the siblings. Holding her hand in the countryside, taking her to the pharmacist for patching-up, cleaning the rag she had bloodied: she read my actions *purely* as motivated by love.

"It's time to sleep, you," Father would say, or, "Go play with the toys, you." Another favorite was, "You're too little for this kind of talk, you." He'd dismiss her with a wave.

That night as he expressed high hopes for his lumber business, we all thought she was asleep in bed. But her voice abruptly rose in the corner of the living room.

"Haven't you smoked enough, you?" Rann parroted reproachfully.

We turned and saw her silhouette against the city lights glittering in from the balcony. It was early autumn, and she was sitting in front of an electric fan. The artificial wind blew her dense black hair about her pale face, giving her the appearance of a vengeful ghost.

Father exploded in silent anger, rising from his chair. He cast about the room, likely seeking a ruler, a flyswatter, anything. He was unwilling to remove his belt in front of us.

I wanted to make sure she left the room so Father wouldn't injure her some other way. Doing the only thing I could think of in the moment, I shouted right back at her.

"Oh, *you're* one to complain! You can't even smell it from over there! You're just jealous you aren't old enough to join us at the big kids' table yet."

Father ceased in his agitated search, resuming his seat. I had managed to soothe him *and* to ensure that he wouldn't raise a hand to Rann.

Izumi sighed, joining in. "Rann, go to sleep. You won't be able to get up for school if you stay with us." She bit her lip. "Father, I think maybe…you *do* smoke too much. It's not healthy. Do you want to die of lung cancer before you can enjoy your lumber fortune?"

Father thrust his cigarette into the tray. "Well, Izumi. You make a very fair point."

It was remarkable, though, that Rann had the nerve to say what none of the rest of us dared to. She had torn a hole in Father's authority, leaving room for the rest of us to speak.

***

At the end of that same year, 1986, the lumber market's economic boom reached its height.

Father, the son of a humble family that had worked the rice paddies for ten generations, was suddenly among the wealthiest men in the nation.

We moved into a luxurious villa in the suburbs. We had curtains embroidered with cherry blossoms hung in front of every window. Seasoned cooks painstakingly prepared our meals.

Father gifted me with an extensive library of Western literature, mostly detective fiction. He had never been able to distinguish between Proust and Conan Doyle. He categorized every Japanese translation of a Western work as *that cultured stuff.*

In the spring of 1987, he enrolled Rann and me in a prestigious boarding school. I started out by verbally defending my little sister's honor, but *words* didn't spare her bruises and scrapes at the hands of bullies. I felt too powerless, and I felt ashamed that my fascination and thrill at the sight of her injuries had only increased. Because my words were ineffective defense *and* because I knew I'd take pleasure on some level, I always found a way to reach her side a moment too late.

Father wanted Fuyutsuki to transfer to my school, too, but she liked her current school and refused to switch. Izumi turned down his suggestion of applying to graduate school overseas, and instead took up administrative work within Father's lumber company.

This was Rann's first year of middle school and my first year of high school, as well as our first time living away from home.

Soon enough, I became an outcast for defending my wayward sister, but I wasn't about to cease coming to her defense. Lither and quicker than many of the other kids my age, who made up the population of Rann's bullies, I started practicing on a punching bag in the school gym.

I got a reputation for following my sister, for being there in time to intervene. I started small—leaving her bullies with black eyes and split lips. *Their* blood, as well as my own from the damage I took, was easier to take pleasure in than Rann's.

While my innate flaw was the cause, I found it convenient to blame the books.

While I devoured Christie and Chandler, the majority of my classmates were making their way through the likes of Joyce and Dostoyevsky, or writers that I inaccurately considered to be their Japanese counterparts—Natsume, Tanizaki, and so on.

I watched my own estrangement with detachment I played off as derision.

"It's just like middle school," I would shrug and say to Fuyutsuki as we talked over the phone. "I'm reading about corpses and alibis while everyone else plays baseball or shares their boring classic novels for class. I'm defending my little sister. It's honorable."

That was just another lie, and a more brazen one than my first tentative omissions.

High school was nothing like middle school for a reason. Another secret crept into my heart during a family trip to Italy that March before school started. I began cutting the inside of my arm when a week or two without any fights with Rann's bullies would pass.

I no longer cared that I suffered from insomnia. Some nights after lights-out, I would keep reading with a flashlight under the quilt. On others, I would lie down, but end up obsessing over Poirot, Marlowe, open wounds, or—not exactly out of the blue—Rann.

Rann's awkwardness and energy remained alarmingly undaunted. Her fatal insensitivity and solitude, I pitied. She felt no pain, couldn't experience what it made me feel.

Four months later, when we all went home for summer break, she grew talkative—outright *noisy*, even. She prattled on and on, complaining about too much schoolwork. She lamented the lack of personal freedom, the gross affectations of politicians' kids, and the incompetent teachers who she found incompetent and doltish. She sounded like *me*.

"Your vocabulary has grown," I interrupted one day as we sat on the floor of her room.

"Oh. Ha, thanks," she replied. "It's all those dull reading assignments, mandatory or optional. I just decided to be competitive—"

"I do hope you're…doing okay, then?" I asked, trying not to be worried and overbearing.

"What do you mean, *doing okay?* I'm splendid! Even all those youngsters with a *refined* upbringing can't compare—"

I sighed and lay down on the tatami. "I'm confused, Rann."

She fell silent for long moments. "Why?" she asked curiously.

"It's like you're not the little sister I've always known. Like you've been hiding."

I looked around her room. The smallest of us all, with blank walls and an austere desk covered in nothing but diligently completed schoolwork.

"You're just pretending to be another person. Deep down, you're still just *Rann*."

"So you don't like the way I talk," she sniffed.

"Can't say I like it," I shot back. "It's vain. It gets you *hurt*. It's no good."

"Izumi likes it. Father, too. Even Fuyutsuki."

"Izumi doesn't notice shit. The only thing Fuyutsuki cares about is video games. As for Father, I'm not sure. Anyway, it's not about what any of them want. It's about what you want, and what you're pretending to be in order to get it. And I don't like that it puts you in danger." Which wasn't strictly true, not when it meant I got to beat her bullies up and get beaten up in kind—experience what she could not.

"You think you know why I changed?" she asked, linking her hands behind her head.

"You talk yourself blue in the face so you don't have enough energy to be your old, klutzy self. If you stop blabbering, you know you'll end up in the school infirmary and get bullied again. If the teachers notice, they might inform Father. Am I right?"

She sighed. "There's this chapter in *Doraemon*, which we're reading for class, where the protagonist uses a 'navel gas machine' to help Nobita feel better. The machine injects a gas into a person's navel so they don't feel pain for thirty minutes. If they find out what I'm like, they'll mock me. *Rann uses navel gas! Where'd you get it, freak? Why do you use navel gas?*"

It was the first time I'd ever heard her imitate the mocking of other people.

"It could easily become *your mom must have a protruding navel*[1]" she went on. "They won't say it in front of teachers, but they'd sure as hell say it behind my back."

"I thought you didn't care what others think about you," I said helplessly.

"Do I look like I don't care what those assholes think?" she retorted, elbowing my side.

"You sure don't care much about what Father thinks. If you cared, you wouldn't have kept doing things to provoke him when you were a little kid. Remember—"

"I care when he insults Mother," she snapped, "even though I never met her. Maybe because I never met her. At least—at least I *can't* feel what she *could*."

"I see," I replied, glancing upward and out the window.

It was typhoon season. The sky was dim, and the trees' branches ebbed and flowed.

"So you…prefer the way I used to talk? The klutz I used to be?" Rann challenged.

---

[1] Japanese equivalent of "son of a bitch"

I considered every possible answer. What could I say to keep her from lashing out, but encourage her that I still cared about her being *who she was*?

"At least you were genuine back then. Not hiding that you're a freak."

Rann did not ask me what I meant by that. She didn't react, either.

"Who am I, Akio?" she asked instead, her tone gone completely flat.

"You're my little sister," I said, wistfully chewing the inside of my lip.

Rann narrowed her eyes. "I want to be in the storm. The typhoon."

"Do you mean you want to face danger? To challenge yourself?"

"Sure," she said glibly. "Why not. Since you miss the *old* me."

"Whatever you choose to do," I said, "I am always on your side. I will always protect you, Rann, and this family's honor. I don't care about my own."

"Even if I end up poking holes in my body? Leaving more scars?"

"Yes. Even if. I'll always be there for you," I swore. *"Always."*

***

Our second and third semesters flew by, during which time my participation in the school orchestra was my social salvation. I made three close friends, who also played strings, and who were all—much to my younger self's surprise—girls.

During the winter break, we formed a quartet, and I was scarcely home. We spent countless hours practicing. We even put together a substantial charity concert with some other students and their parents, who of course carried significant influence.

Thinking back, one motivation behind my devotion to the quartet was to avoid getting in scrapes with Rann's bullies. It was difficult to deny my desires, but I made an effort by diving headlong into music. My constant fights, and the increasing severity of injuries to my opponents, meant dishonor to my family.

According to Fuyutsuki, Rann had gone back to her old self—laconic and restless. She was the only member of my family who did not show up at the charity concert that winter.

It turned out that Izumi had developed a substantial grudge.

"I don't understand," she said spitefully. "Akio is *clearly* Rann's favorite, but, for some reason, she wouldn't come. I wonder why."

"That's enough, Izumi," Father said, the smoke from his cigarette curling in the freezing air. "There's no hope for that one anyway."

"It bothers me, how she never learns gratitude," Izumi continued. "What would she have become without this family? Without *Akio*?"

I felt a swell of loss. In defending her honor, I had somehow defended only my own.

***

My father cornered me for a talk in his study during February of 1988.

"I talk to Izumi because she understands me. She knows my business and my difficulties," he explained. "She gives very good advice. Now, I talk to Fuyutsuki because she's undisciplined. Always has been. I never talked to you, Akio, because you're such a good kid. Talented. I want to protect your peace of mind as much as I can. But this time…" He frowned and sucked on his cigarette. "I need your help. It's about…*that one*."

Rann had recently made some more enemies. One day, a group of girls held her down on the floor. The leader had sat on her chest and held a ballpoint pen to her cheek, threatening to poke her face. Defiant, Rann had grabbed the leader's hand and pushed the pen right through.

I'd been on a school trip the day it happened, so I hadn't been able to intervene. On hearing about it, I had tried to imagine what I would have done. The result was a bloodbath. I wondered if I could have killed the leader of those girls in the moment.

"Imagine how disturbed those girls must be!" Father said as he pressed the remaining cigarette into the ashtray on his ebony desk. "Those are the daughters of Treasury Officials. Can you imagine? I worked my ass off trying to please those people, but now *that one* is tormenting their kids." He shook his head. "She didn't even cry when she was born, did you know that? They took her out, and she was quiet. She burped when the doctor smacked her. We didn't think much of it. I eventually recognized she'd be a time bomb, but *this*!"

I nodded as sympathetically as I could manage. I didn't want to risk betraying my thoughts of fatal vengeance on girls who were mere children in comparison to myself.

Father lit another cigarette and pointed at me.

"Akio," he said, "you're the one she listens to. Talk to her about this. Make her aware of her bad manners. I'm counting on you."

That night I found her sitting in the middle of the huge lawn behind the villa.

"So," I said as I sat down beside her, "tell me about this whole ballpoint pen thing."

She turned to me, and I saw the patch-bandage on her cheek. I imagined the shape of the stitched wound under the patch, quivering with excitement. Imagined killing the girl who had inflicted such a grotesque injury upon her, and injuring the others.

Self-control, I told myself. *Like the day of the storm.*

"Shameful," I said, "the way those girls attacked you out of the blue. I wish I had been there to help. What do you think was the trigger?"

"It was right after our literature exam." Rann turned her eyes back to the starless night sky. "They were talking about an obscure passage. I knew they didn't understand it, so I cut in. They knew I was right. I guess that pissed them off."

"But the way they carried it so far…" I cringed to cover my thrill at imagining the entire scenario. "That was too much."

"Not for them," Rann laughed. "They come from a long line of college graduates, whereas we come from a long line of peasants. How dare I correct *them*?"

I said nothing, hoping that my silence continued to speak purely as condemnation.

"Akio," Rann said, "do you still have those flight dreams? Where you take a running leap and glide over people's heads—over skyscrapers, even?"

I turned to look at her. There was a dreamy expression on her face.

"I haven't dreamed in ages," I confessed. "Why do you ask?"

"When you flew like that, did you feel the wind on your face?"

"No, I don't think I did. All I remember is the amazing view."

"When I have them," Rann said, "I feel the wind more than I see the view. An overwhelming, obliterating gust of wind, blowing hard against my skin. That wind is the only thing in the world when I dream. I think"—she turned to me, her eyes suddenly brimming with expectant thrill—"*that* is the kind of storm I'm really after."

"Where do you expect to find that storm," I asked mildly, to deflect her more serious intentions, "*except* in your dreams? Surely not in pissing off more government VIPs' kids, I hope."

"You know what's the funniest part about the whole ballpoint pen thing?" Rann laughed. "That girl was so scared that she wet her pants while she sat on me! Well, not so funny when I had to wash my uniform. But you get the idea."

"Why do you want to scare them like that anyway?" I asked. "It requires you to hurt yourself, and you know we don't want you to get hurt. I don't want you to get hurt."

Rann's smile disappeared. "I thought you wanted me to be more like my old self. *Authentic.* Anyway, they said our mother must've had a protruding navel. They deserve it."

I didn't know what to say, but it seemed I'd failed in deterring her from her course.

"It's okay," she said. "It's an injury to Mother, not to me. She can't feel it, either."

"But I thought you were determined to defend Mother's honor," I chided.

Rann shrugged. "I like to imagine she sacrificed her life so I could live. It's a lie, though. She died for herself, not any of us. If she'd loved us, she would've stayed home that day."

I lost my words again, listening intently, waiting for another shot.

"But you're right," she sighed. "My storm's not those girls, and it's not Mother."

We were silent for a while. The evening breeze ruffled our hair about our faces.

"Akio," Rann said, loudly so I'd hear her over the wind, "I'll continue to look for that storm. When I find it, I'll dive right in. Even if it tears me to pieces and scatters me all over this island country, or holds me aloft and tosses me down like a rag doll. Will you still be on my side?"

The blast of excitement in me was pure, and the gale was *electrifying*.

I wanted to see what her weird sharpness would continue to do to the unsuspecting world. What my defense of her honor would continue to do to the world, come to it.

"Yes, I will always be with you," I said, knowing I would always follow.

***

Rann was not just sharp, a force to be reckoned with. She was unstoppable.

Father called me into his study for a second, third, and fourth time, enraged.

I told him that I had tried my best, but that Rann would have no way but her own.

Father exhaled and watched his smoke spread across the room.

"Okay," he would say, "I believe you. Just—keep trying!"

Then, he would release Rann from the damp, windowless basement, which was where she had been grounded for several days. She never showed signs of suffering.

"Still, I'd *prefer* detention in the school office," she complained to me, no more than mildly irritated. "I'll have to repeat a grade if this keeps happening."

"They're too scared to keep you in the school office," I replied as I closed the basement door behind her. "You're too authentic even for the headmaster."

Rann did not end up repeating. She scored high on every end-of-year exam, and even her attendance surpassed the required minimum.

One afternoon in her last year of middle school, in the well-trimmed woods behind the school's immaculate buildings, the mayor's daughter cornered Rann with a number of her friends. The brawl ended with Rann punching the mayor's daughter, giving her a bloody nose.

This time, I was there, too. I got in the next blow, dislocating the leader's jaw and knocking out one of her molars. The leader's friends had to pull me off of her.

I studied the bruising on both of our knuckles and wrists on our way home from the police station. There had been an undeniable thrill in being sent there together, as accomplices.

"Is this your storm yet?" I whispered. "Did I help you get what you wanted? I meant what I said when I'd always be with you."

Rann brought her hand in front of her eyes. She clenched her fingers into a tight fist, and then extended them as far as possible, reminding me of the dishrag I'd once washed out.

"No," Rann replied. "Not at all."

A few days later, Father summoned me to his study.

"Rann. *Storm.* She's the storm that's gonna tear apart all the hard work I've done. What was your mother *thinking* when she came up with that name?"

Names mattered to my father. His own name, Hiroshi, meant *large, extensive, having a vast heart.* He considered his name one of the most important factors behind his success, and had rummaged through dictionaries in search of names for his children.

So there was Izumi, mountain spring, the first daughter; Fuyutsuki, winter moon, the second daughter; and Akio, born with the rising sun, the third child and only son—me.

But something happened in the three years between my birth and Rann's. Something that had left Father loath to name her, loath to be present when she was born.

"Izumi was the only one there when Rann came," Fuyutsuki told me as we stood side by side on the rooftop of a science building at her university, leaning against the protective wire netting. "How funny. Izumi was only ten, and had to lock us in our bedroom at that sordid apartment so we wouldn't…I don't know, blow up the kitchen or something."

"I remember," I said in admiration. "You almost throttled me to death."

She laughed. "Well, at least I learned to keep my shit in check as I grew."

"Yeah. You found television and Nintendo Famicom more exciting than a snotty little brother. I know all of that. Let's go back to what happened at the hospital."

"So the doctors came out and told Izumi the baby was a girl, and Izumi called Father's office. She thought Father sounded cross at first. Interrupted for no good reason. 'So what? What do you want from me?' he asked. Izumi was taken aback, and just asked if he had come up with a name for the baby girl. 'Tell your mother to think of something, I don't know, maybe about her hometown,' Father said, and hung up. Izumi delivered the message."

I looked up to the pale grey sky. "I just realized I know next to nothing about Mother. I don't even know where she came from."

"Yeah." Fuyutsuki rolled her eyes. "You found that chubby Belgian detective with a funny mustache more exciting than Mother. I've more or less looked into her past."

"What did you find?" I decided to let her remark about my fascination with Poirot go.

"Mother came from a seaside town where typhoons lift fishing boats into the sky. When Father met her in the city, she was singing in a cabaret. Actually, she was quite the star. No idea why she would marry him. He had a stable job, but was making even less money."

"Maybe they were in love."

"Ha. That's funny. Didn't know you are the romantic type. Anyway, Mother said, let's call her Rann. Rann of the Windstorm."

"She actually said *windstorm*?"

"Remember the biker gang?"

"Yeah. A few weeks after Rann was born, one of the Windstorm bikers crushed Mother's windshield with a hammer and threw a homemade grenade at the car…"

I shivered, just barely hiding the thrill imagining it gave me.

"Did you never wonder why it happened?" Fuyutsuki asked.

"I thought it was just something that outlaw bikers do."

"Oh, Akio." Fuyutsuki stared at me. "So that's how you've explained the death of your mother to yourself? They say ignorance is bliss, but you're just…cold-blooded."

"Says the one who tried to throttle me multiple times," I shot back, unnerved at her perceptiveness. "Come on, I was three when she died. I don't have the faintest memory of her. I'm asking you only because I want to find out why Father always treats Rann that way."

Fuyutsuki turned around and locked her fingers onto the crisscross wires of the netting.

"Mother actually disappeared from home," she said, "when you were about one. Father had neither the money, nor the time to search for her. She reappeared a little more than a year later, though, and Father welcomed her with open arms and tears running down his face. Nine months later, Rann was born. But during that period, Father discovered a message Mother received from a biker in the Windstorm gang. In the letter, the kid mentioned their relationship and a baby boy they had had together. Father confronted her, and she admitted it was true."

"Wait. We have a half brother somewhere out there?"

"Yes."

"And Rann could be the child of that biker as well."

"According to Izumi, Rann looks just like Mother. Inconclusive."

"Why did the biker end up murdering her?" I asked, hoping for details.

"Maybe he felt betrayed. Insulted. You know, he's a gangster. What troubles me more is why Mother would go to that mountain pass. It was practically Windstorm's realm. Were there threats? Blackmail? Did it involve our brother? Had she gone after him?" Fuyutsuki sighed when she saw me staring at her, waiting for an answer. "It was fifteen years ago, Akio. There's no way we can possibly find out."

My mind buzzed with possibilities. I needed to share this secret with my accomplice.

"Should I tell Rann?"

"I guess Rann has realized a lot on her own over the years, but...I don't think we should tell her anything. Given the way she is."

"How did you get to know all of this? Father wouldn't have told you."

"Father told Izumi. You know how they always have those one-on-one deep talks in his study with the door closed. When those talks are too much to for Izumi, she tells me."

"Seems like Izumi trusts you more than I ever imagined."

Fuyutsuki turned to me and smiled. "What are siblings for?"

I pictured her smile and watched Father torture his cigarette.

Siblings are scapegoats, Fuyutsuki. For amusement. I thought you knew.

"I'm sorry things didn't work out." I put my palm over Father's warm, greasy fist.

Father did not raise his head. "Do you *know*, Akio?"

"Yes, I do know," I said.

"I'm such a fool. It's been so long. I should have remarried. Should've sent *that one* to an orphanage. Why didn't I? Tell me, Akio."

I felt his hand tremble with suffering and delighted in it. I hated him for the harm he'd always done to Rann. He deserved to suffer for what he had done, and I was justified in enjoying *this* particular suffering even if no blood or broken bones were involved.

"I don't know, Father," I said, "but I have another question."

He looked up at me in resignation. "Then get on with it."

"Since you always knew Rann can't feel pain, why did you beat her? There's no way it was going to work. You wasted your time. You dishonored her *and* yourself."

Father started sobbing, and I delighted in that, too. I had won.

"I've got to do something," he said. "Akio, what should I do?"

***

That night, I sat bolt upright in bed, shivering in a cold sweat.

I'd been dreaming, but couldn't remember. Anger gripped me at the knowledge that I had made Father feel anguish and guilt, but apparently not enough to let Rann out of the cellar.

I tottered down the stairs with the cellar key in my sweaty fist.

As I pushed the cellar door open, I saw the naked incandescent bulb hanging from a worn wire duct-taped to the ceiling. I spotted the dusty table on which Rann had piled her homework during the semester, and the old chair covered in peeling red leather.

But I could not see Rann, which made me frantic with concern.

"Rann?" I hissed. "Where are you?"

I heard the shuffle of her clothes from a corner of the room. When my sight adjusted to the darkness, I made out the outline of her squatting in the corner with her back toward me.

I slowly closed the door behind me, shivering at a high-pitched squeak of horror.

Rann turned around and slowly walked into the light of the incandescent bulb. She had a rat by the neck, squeezing it between her thumb and forefinger.

"Gotcha," she said, her pearly teeth gleaming between her parched lips.

Her arms were covered in scratches and puncture wounds from the rat.

Without hurrying, she lifted her left hand to grab the head of the suffocating animal.

Calmly, I waited for the crisp snap of the creature's spine.

Rann did not disappoint. I grinned at her as the creature's life drained.

I took her upstairs. As I rinsed cleaned her arms in the kitchen sink, she started talking about the time we went to a famed seafood restaurant. The fish's tail had twitched when the chef gutted it; she and I had both been watching.

"Even a fish can feel," Rann said. "Evolutionarily speaking, I'm lower than a fish."

"No, Rann, you're not," I said adamantly. "You're human, just like the rest of us."

"I don't understand, Akio," she said, oddly disheartened. "People are connected by pain. But me? I don't know when to say what, how to react. I'm doomed to be an outcast."

"Listen to yourself, Rann," I said. "You have human thoughts all the same."

"But why am I the one?" she asked, her voice a monotone.

I shook my head in silence, and then dressed her wounds.

Under the harsh yellow light of the kitchen bulb, she almost looked like the wood-carved statue of the Kannon bodhisattva. Inhuman, untouchable. *Unstoppable.*

"We're going to the hospital tomorrow," I said as I led her reluctantly back into the cellar, "but, tonight, I'm here to tell you something about Mother."

Rann looked straight to me, eyes inscrutably sharp.

2

Not long after that, Rann ran away from home.

She was seventeen. It was two years after the latest and bloodiest incident with the mayor's daughter, and the autumn of her second year in high school.

Rann ran away from home with a teenage biker, but nobody reported it to the police.

She had been gone for two days before I found out; I had been beside myself with worry.

That was the evening of my annual concert, the concert in which I always played First Chair.

"We didn't want to distress you," Izumi said. "We know you love Rann."

"It's more important that you don't mess up the performance," Father said.

"This is bullshit," Fuyutsuki whispered. *"You* know where to find her."

Later that night, roaming alone in the outskirts of the city in search of her, I saw the headlight of a bullet train as it shot across the low-hanging overpass.

The train brought a roaring gale. There was a tugging motion, the ghost of shock, the fluttering of my hair even though I was in no way close to the track.

The train's windowpanes shook uncontrollably, as if a demented horde of inmates was gathered inside the long line of grey apartments facing the railway, grabbing the metal window frames and shaking, dying for a chance to get out.

It was only after the train had gone that human sounds started to reemerge: shouting, drunken swearing, breaking of glass or porcelain.

That was when I knew she'd found her storm, furious I wouldn't be there to see. But my feet had carried me there—always destined to follow her, to be with her no matter what.

Rann had told me about the home of her biker boyfriend a week ago over the phone. He lived alone. It was a small suite with windows facing a certain railroad track, on the top floor of a five-story building. The neighborhood was inhabited by laborers and novice gangsters and who-knew-what-else.

There were five locks on the apartment door, graffiti on the dirty chalk walls of the corridor, and a barely functional air-conditioning unit. At night, if the blinds were left open, passing trains caused glowing bars of light to flash across the walls.

"Like in a film noir classic," Rann had said, thrilled, appealing to my love of mysteries.

I turned at a T-junction and walked down another narrow street, still gazing at the apartment buildings and wondering how Rann could possibly sleep with so much noise.

That was when I saw a figure appear from an alley across the street.

A high-school boy dressed in black leather biker gear strolled along with hunched shoulders and hands in his pockets. The right side of his face was disfigured, perhaps burn-scarred.

That one might know something, I thought. *Maybe I can threaten it out of him.*

I walked right up to him and said, "I'm looking for my sister. She's been hanging around here lately, so don't lie to me. She's seventeen, about this tall, and…"

The boy stood his ground and gave me a dubious head-to-toe.

I still wore my bespoke concert suit and carried my violin case.

"The hell are you talking about?" the boy sneered. "Get lost! Go to the police!"

"We can't go to the police!" I sneered back, emboldened, wielding my violin case. "Do you know what I really have in here? I don't think I have to tell you. The most you have is a knife. Do you really want to try your luck?"

"It's not like I know every girl who's hitting on bikers around here," he countered.

"I'll pay you," I said, grabbing him by his collar, "and let you live."

"Don't touch me!" he growled. "I could knife you before you shoot."

"I'll pay you anything you want," I repeated, making as if to open my violin case. "But if I have to shoot you, what good would the money do you then?"

"Then tell me more about what she looks like," the boy muttered, as if I had a point.

"Seventeen," I repeated. "About this tall. Lean girl, but muscular. She wears her long hair up in a ponytail. There's a scar on her cheek, from a stab wound. When she left home, she was wearing a short-sleeved black sailor suit with a crimson tie."

"Scar on her left cheek," he said, relaxing somewhat. "She's quite new around here, no? Yes, I think I know her. Lucky for you."

"Tell me where she is," I demanded.

"Payment first," he said, eyes narrowed.

"This violin is worth a fortune," I said. "You really thought I had a gun, didn't you? You're a gullible fool, not as tough as you look. Sell it."

The boy huffed in distaste. "On second thought, I don't want your money."

"What?" I blurted, wondering if I'd misheard. I wanted to punch him in the jaw like I'd done with Rann's schoolmate—only I wanted to keep punching, and punching, and *punching*. I wanted his face to be nothing but bone and blood.

"I don't want you rich people's dirty money," he jeered. "Just play me a song."

While it would ruin my tough image, it seemed like my best shot at finding Rann. I told myself that was more important than punching him to death.

With bullet trains occasionally passing, and apartment residents hurling abuse and beer bottles down at us, I played the first three minutes of Vaughan Williams's "The Lark Ascending."

The biker boy seemed to enjoy it. He closed his eyes and linked his hands behind his head, fingers tangled in his hair—a pose that reminded me of Rann on the day of the typhoon.

The boy told me what I needed to know as I packed my violin away.

Rann was in a relationship with one of the leaders of the Halcyon biker gang. Most members dressed in blue, but the color of the second-in-command—Rann's boyfriend—was aquamarine. Both the leader and the second lived in apartments nearby, so the Halcyons had a regular gathering point in an underground pub around the T-junction.

"You're lucky. If you just wait around here, maybe they'll show up," the boy said. "Who knows. Sometimes people are destined to meet."

"Maybe I was meant to meet *you* here today," I said.

"Come on," he snapped. "All these manners? It's making me sick. What's your name, by the way?"

"Why do you need to know?" I said threateningly.

The boy laughed. "So that I can boast to other thugs when you become famous and go on TV. You dumb? It's so obvious."

"My name is Kimura Akio," I said. "What's *your* name?"

"Asuka Shinn," he replied. "Just call me Asuka."

"Asuka? *Flying* bird. That's not a common last name. Is your family from Nara county? There's an Asuka Temple there."

"Dunno. Probably made up. I never met my parents."

"I'm sorry," I said, wondering why he'd got past my defenses.

"Rich kids are *never* sorry," he sighed. "I gotta get going."

"I wouldn't delay you further," I said, as if *letting* him go.

"Hey, if your sister decides to stay, we might see each other again," Asuka said.

"She can't," I said, compelled to scowl at him. *Because she's my storm, mine.*

"Shame." Asuka shrugged. "You seem like a good brother. The Halcyons' second is a good brother, too. You'll get along just..." His voice fell as something distracted him.

I followed his gaze. A little girl in a halcyon-blue dress was playing hopscotch alone on the crosswalk. She looked to be about five. Her eyes gleamed under the streetlamp.

"Speak of the devil," Asuka whispered to me. "That's his little sister. Seems their old woman is drunk again. I'd better go. No good if I'm seen with the brat. He'd think I'm scheming something."

Little sister. The little sister of the man who had taken Rann away from me. Because he'd taken her, didn't he deserve to suffer? Didn't his family deserve dishonor?

That was when the first faint rumbling of motorcycles started to sound. When the sound approached with ever-increasing speed, I could clearly see both the rider and her path.

"Watch out!" Asuka shouted, but I dragged him back before he could warn the little girl again. I knew what the girl and her family deserved, and I would see it done.

I released him, watching with detachment as the bike roared around the corner. The rider lost control, ejected with dramatic and impressive force.

The bike made impact, the sickening splatter followed by an explosion.

My ears were ringing as, thrilled, I raised my head to find Asuka gone.

Not far from the slain girl's remains, I saw Rann lying on the ground. She was trying to prop herself up on both arms. She was still wearing the black sailor suit—now covered in dirt—with only the most basic protective gear, and no helmet.

I heard the growl of a swarm of motorcycles approaching and knew it was the Halcyons in hot pursuit. I scrambled to my feet and rushed to her, not inclined to let them win. I wouldn't let them take my beloved little sister away from me again.

As I draped one of her arms around my neck and helped her to her feet, I saw the deep, bleeding scrapes on her left cheek, forearm, and leg. Gravel and debris stuck to her flesh.

I was immersed in the thrill of it: a volcanic spring, its electric heat engulfing me.

No way, I told myself, a token protest. *You can't. You shouldn't. Don't you dare.*

But I smiled anyway, no longer inclined to hide.

When I did, Rann was smiling back—an incandescent smile that pulled at the scrape on her face. She pinched my arm hard, made me feel what she could not. Pain as expression of love. She understood me now, or perhaps she always had.

Rann had flown as I'd flown in my dreams, and I would follow.

So, how's that for a storm? Rann's flashing eyes asked.

I picked up the violin case, and we ran, we ran, we *ran*.

R-15

When the hemispherical screen displaying the Cyborg Health Monitoring System started flashing, the scientist was fast asleep on her desk. It was littered with empty, single-use syringes that once contained doses of nutrients and stimulants.

Over the past seven months, the scientist had been diligently working to rehabilitate *Kyllikki*, the massive Saarian spacecraft whose internal circuits had been obliterated the last time her son went berserk. She had little time and energy to spend tracking down her son.

Despite having lost the trace on its target's whereabouts, the CHMS seemed to be functioning perfectly. Even if it did not know where the scientist's son *was*, it nonetheless produced data promising that he was in fine condition and high spirits.

That was enough for the scientist. She still regretted that she'd been unable to dissuade her son from his quest—which was doomed, desperate, and illegal. But she had reconsidered.

Now, the scientist wanted nothing but success and emotional fulfillment for her son. She held herself aloft in a soft, idyllic dream. She was contemplating the idyllic years they'd spent on their homeworld, Farmind, when a brash alarm sounded from within *Kyllikki*.

WARNING! UNSPECIFIED DAMAGE! FUEL LEAKAGE! FIND SHELTER!

The scientist woke from her dozing with a start, blinded by the messages' rapid flashing on her screen. She realized she'd left the monitor plugged into *Kyllikki*'s central system.

Retreating, the scientist hid behind the tall pane of reinforced glass near her console. She watched the screen expand, burst, and spurt sweltering black mucus from *Kyllikki*'s fuel lines.

This reminded the scientist of her son's early days as a cyborg. He had lost control of his burgeoning power and burst his energy core, raining down depressurized droplets of fuel.

The scientist remained behind her glass shield for a while, gasping with the tears that coursed down her cheeks. Eventually, she stood up, made her way across the fuel-slicked floor, and sat down at her console. With apprehension, she relaunched the Intergalactic Messaging Interface for the first time in seven months.

Floods of unread messages poured in. Among them, she instantly spotted two requests that had been sent from Pohjola seven months earlier. The blunt subject lines indicated that they were concerned with her fugitive cyborg son's apparent and continuing misconduct.

REQUEST-INFO: Key to Deactivation of Organismal Firewall against EMM

REQUEST-SUMMONS: Former Operator of L-KMN, come to Pohjola ASAP

Pohjola. That was where the trace she'd fixed on her son had gone silent. Therefore, it was the latest-known stop on his journey of willful destruction.

The scientist wiped her eyes and sniffed. She tugged her limp spacesuit from the back of the chair and donned it. She climbed into her compact, conical shuttle and set off for Pohjola.

When she reached it, she saw that the space station lay in a state of partial ruin. Construction Drones carried bundles of materials needed for repair, scurrying about and filling in the yawning cracks and fissures that threatened to admit the terrors of deep space.

"You are finally here," intoned Louhi, the AI Executive stationed in Pohjola's central shaft. "I am obliged to inform you of your Cyborg L-KMN's misconduct, as well as the corresponding charges. In requesting information on the Crossbow of Hiisi, L-KMN is in direct violation of Intergalactic Constitution Item 15, subsections 68 – 137. It was scheduled for detention, but escaped before receiving judgment from the Interstellar Weaponry Committee. By inflicting damages on Pohjola during its escape, it expanded its criminal record. It has been placed on the Intergalactic Offender List, and is now legally under the jurisdiction of the Committee. Please note that, as its *absent* operator, you have surrendered all authority over L-KMN."

The scientist went weak in the knees and fell before Louhi, struggling for breath.

"Although you have in no observable way assisted L-KMN, and the results of my analysis categorize this incident as a typical case of Berserk Action," Louhi continued, "the Committee has found it necessary to place you on the Caution List. This action has been taken with regard to L-KMN's disappearance from the Intergalactic Tracer Map, as well as your nonresponse to the Committee's request for L-KMN's Deactivation Key. Our snipers have sedative darts aimed at you as we speak, but that may be excessive. My analysis indicates that your actions are explicable. The first few cases of L-KMN's Berserk Actions resulted in biosphere destruction on your home planet of Farmind, which accounts for your failure to assist L-KMN. Unfortunately, L-KMN attacked Saari next, where it obtained the legendary spacecraft *Kyllikki*. Even with the Intergalactic Unity's technological assistance, it has been impossible to locate. My analysis suggests you knew the extent of L-KMN's destructive intent and the risk of Berserk Action. You may even know it seeks the Crossbow of Hiisi. At minimum, you know Pohjola has jurisdiction over Hiisi, which is a State of the Intergalactic Unity, unlike the Unincorporated Territories of Farmind and Saari. Catching our attention would have resulted in swift judgment, so you have been hiding in *Kyllikki* for the past seven months. Am I wrong?"

The scientist stared up at Louhi, unable to speak. It was not wrong.

"I will take your nonresponse as confirmation. As for my request for L-KMN's Deactivation Key, it was a default message. I did not expect you would comply. I accessed hospital records on Farmind and learned that your biological son was paralyzed during the War. You mechanized him and renamed him. You refuse to let him be paralyzed again, this time through Electromagnetic Manipulation. I ask you again: am I wrong?"

In response to the scientist's silence, Louhi seemed to sigh in exasperation.

"Personally, I sympathize with the difficulties you Farminders experienced after the Incorporation. I would even commend you for the exceptional achievement of creating such a powerful cyborg. However, L-KMN has proven itself uncontrollable. It must stand before the Committee and face judgment. If you agree to assist in our search and succeed, you will be removed from the Caution List. You are a specialist in the recovery and repair of Saarian technology. With your knowledge of Saari and your mastery of cyborg conversion, you have a much higher chance of bringing L-KMN back to the Committee."

The scientist considered Louhi's expressive constellation of blinking lights.

"If you refuse, you will be moved to the Offender List instantly and detained to await judgment before the Humanoid Mechanization Committee. You have a choice. You must have left *Kyllikki* and come out of hiding for a reason. There must be something that my research has not uncovered. The important thing is your presence. *Choose.*"

An eye-level holoscreen appeared before the scientist. She raised a trembling finger and pressed *ACCEPT.* Without a word, she rose and returned to her shuttle.

Back in the privacy of her own space, the scientist injected herself with a dose of stimulant.

Next, she patched her personal computer into Pohjola's network and perused the surveillance files for a while. What she found confirmed every last one of her suspicions.

Louhi had told her two lies. One was that her son had escaped Pohjola; the other was that they had no idea where to find him.

Louhi must have told the scientist's son a lie concerning how to access the Crossbow of Hiisi, to lure him away and to preserve Pohjola. Although it was impossible to hack into the AI Executive's memory files, the scientist was able to delve deeper into Pohjola's surveillance.

She found the files from seven months ago: her son's arrival and the havoc that followed.

The scientist watched as Pohjola's outer shield was blown away, as he approached with a comet tail of sparks trailing behind. She watched every housing capsule burst in a spray of humanoid limbs and entrails as her son released the residential area's pressure valve. She watched as the remains were vaporized to crimson mist, and then faded to nothing.

The scientist watched as her son floated before Louhi and his judgmental constellation of lights, full of determined rage, a young god of destruction. He was radiant.

Tears were rolling down the scientist's cheeks again, to her shame. She barely made out Louhi's response in the recording as she continued to watch:

You are in the wrong place. As of the present point in time, we here on Pohjola have nothing to do with the Crossbow of Hiisi. We have disavowed all access for the sake of this space station's safety. You must travel to Artificial Star R-15, at the center of Joutsen Galaxy #000000. R-15 is the key to the Crossbow of Hiisi.

The scientist had no knowledge of a Joutsen galaxy with designation #000000.

She typed the text into the Intergalactic Search Engine: *0 results. Are you searching for...*

Next, the scientist navigated her shuttle to the space station of Metsä, which hosted the largest library and archives in the Unity. The aim of automatic sniper rifles followed her from the entrance to the nearest inquiry kiosk.

With shaking fingers, the scientist typed: *Joutsen #000000. 0 results. Are you searching for...*

Request access to classified material, she typed on a hunch.

The kiosk's screen requested an ID Number, which she lacked.

When it requested a Guarantor, she typed *Louhi of Pohjola.*

Access denied, said the kiosk's screen, maddeningly adamant.

The scientist plugged in her rerouting device, the one she'd used to rifle through Pohjola's surveillance files, in a last-ditch attempt to gain unauthorized access.

Access denied. Warning: You have overstepped...

She rushed back into her shuttle and took off.

How would her son have known where to go?

Where would he have sought out the answer?

The scientist traveled to Saari. She tramped through the ruins of its dead civilization, searching for access to the Library of Tie.

Twenty years ago, she and her son had strolled side by side under the library's grand dome, enthralled by the elaborate engravings on its pillars made of conglomerated rare-earth sand.

What are you thinking, L? You look deep in thought.

If the Saarians were so advanced, why did they die off?

We don't know, but research is ongoing. There are theories. Historical records reveal evidence of a cataclysmic civil war. Demographic study suggests that they may have abused certain eugenic techniques. Geological findings suggest climate change was in play. Maybe they didn't die off. Maybe they migrated to another corner of the universe. They had the technology. Remember Kyllikki? *Or maybe they've become part of this barren landscape. The core of Saarian technology is bringing inorganic substances to life.*

Huh. Maybe one day they'll jump out and accuse us of stealing their knowledge!

That's funny, L. Remember that the Saarians are teachers—even parents of a sort—to us Farminders. They left behind so much for us to learn.

Twenty years ago, the Intergalactic Fleet had arrived, conquered, and asserted dominance.

The Territorial Resource Management Bureau had developed Saari into a rare-earth mine, taken down the glass domes, carried away the sand pillars, and left behind long deep ditches.

In retribution, the scientist's son had returned to Saari. He had massacred the Bureau employees and blasted every settlement, sweeping over Saari in less than a week.

But the formidable Library of Tie was still there.

At the onset of Bureau interference, the scientist had joined a group of Farmind scholars to plead for preservation of Saarian relics. They had only managed to preserve Tie and *Kyllikki*.

The scientist pushed open the library's reinforced glass doors, to discover that more than half of its organic documents had been vaporized during her son's catastrophic visit. Among the remnants, she found no reference to Joutsen Galaxy #000000.

Fearful, the scientist climbed back into her shuttle and headed to Farmind.

There might be something left in her ex-colleagues' notes. She hadn't revisited Farmind since her son vaporized its last traces of life.

Farmind was the planet closest to Saari. She could rest and think about where to go next.

Soon, the scientist was back in Kuu, the university town where she had grown up. She had gone to school there, met her husband there, raised her son there. She had even taught there.

Nothing was left. Grey buildings, burnt earth, lifeless water. She used fuel from her shuttle to power the computers left behind by those who once taught with her, worked on the same research projects with her, published papers with her.

They had all perished in the War of Self-Defense, as guerrillas, at Intergalacian hands.

And there was nothing, not even a trace, in their files mentioning Joutsen #000000.

The scientist wandered into the ruins of the hospital. There, her son once lay paralyzed among his fellow wounded Self-Defense soldiers.

Is destruction the only eternal thing, mother? Is death the only end?

There was a sunlit corner where her son had asked his doomed questions.

I want to become eternal, mother. I shall become the only end.

The scientist walked to the abandoned corner and saw a pool of clear water gathered in the slanted wooden floorboards. The wooden planks had turned black where the water touched their surface fibers, and she spotted something against the blackness.

The scientist lowered her head, until she could see green spheres of algae in the water. She wept again, her tears viscous with the stimulants she'd injected to stave off exhaustion.

She finally had the courage to answer her son's volley of doomed questions: *No.*

Under some nearby debris, she found the touchscreen tablet on which her son had often tried to scribble with a pen in his mouth. She put it on a charging station and booted it up, recognizing the shining Intergalactic Medicine logo.

She opened the file titled with her son's name and tried to identify his mouth-writing:

I hate   dead lost   where
*   go die   mother   destroy*
*   I can't   Saari Farmind*
* home   Kyllikki live*
*   in shit   JOUTSEN*
*   die   #000000*

The scientist let the tablet slip from her hands and shatter on the floorboards.

She staggered back to her shuttle and took off, heading toward *Kyllikki* where she had left it stationed in orbit above Kuu. In the Saarian spacecraft, she activated the pilot's console and entered *Joutsen* #000000—by handwriting it, using the Intergalactic Alphabet.

The three-dimensional map on the far wall automatically highlighted Kaleva, the home galaxy of the solar system containing Farmind and Saari.

The scientist was drowning in a tide of questions.

What did her findings mean? Had the Saarians created the Intergalactic language? Were the Intergalacians of Saarian ancestry? If so, why did they seek to destroy *Kyllikki*? Had her son researched *Kyllikki* on his own? How long had he known?

I've got to find my son, the scientist told herself. *I've got to find my son first.*

She zoomed in on the three-dimensional map, locating the heart of Joutsen #000000—a supermassive black hole labeled *Tuonela* in Intergalactic.

The scientist did not know how to start up *Kyllikki*, not for all her trying. She only knew that the hollow shaft with a pointed end seemed to be connected with the engine—through an exquisite instrument whose use probable use genetic analysis.

There is no other way, the scientist thought as she pricked her palm on the shaft's point.

My son is my only family. My son is my only people.

As the scientist's blood oozed into the shaft, *Kyllikki*'s engine roared to life.

Every drop of fuel that had burst through the hemispherical screen at her console swam back inside the pipeline, the leakage restoring itself like a wound healing.

The fragments yet to be repaired floated to where they should be. The panel of reinforced glass restored itself as a second layer to the panoramic window.

The hungry spacecraft tilted its head, detecting the sun of Farmind and Saari. It leaped forward, gulping the gas and light of its homeworld's star.

The scientist held on with all her might, disoriented.

Kyllikki shot through space and time to a location near Tuonela, where the black hole's accretion disk loomed forbiddingly.

Through the panoramic window, the scientist saw a whole fleet of Intergalactic ships. Some were damaged and some intact. They had formed a matrix, which was swiftly closing in on a minute humanoid figure ablaze at its center.

Kyllikki glided right through, breaking the matrix without taking damage, but it was still too late.

The scientist watched her godlike son sense her presence. He gave her one last, beatific smile before the myriad cubic cuts on his body began to show.

Her son's body splintered into shining fragments, sucked into the spinning disk of Tuonela.

Kyllikki plunged into the black hole's perilous rapids. Using the spacecraft's debris catcher, the scientist fished for splinters of her son, gathering them one by one.

Exhausted, she slid to the floor.

With limp legs and trembling hands, the scientist knelt before her son's remains, trying to piece him back together. A hand, a toe, a shoulder blade. A knot of entrails, a vertebra, a rib. Plastic sinews, metallic muscles, electronic nerves.

The scientist recalled the long months she'd carried the boy inside her, and then the years she spent building him a body of Saarian mechanization.

My son was born twice, she thought. *Now must be the third time.*

The end of their fateful last talk flashed in her head again, excruciating:

I want to become eternal, mother.

I don't want to be eternal. Can't we go back to the normal family we were?

Go back, mother? What are you talking about? There is no way back.

There is! If you're willing to hold my hand again and follow me, just like when you were little. Because you are little now, L. You've just been born a second time.

I can't take your hand anymore, nor will I follow.

L—!

I will see you at our only end, mother. I know this now. Is destruction the only eternal thing? I want to become eternal, so that perhaps I might prevent future harm to us.

No, L—destruction is not *the only eternal thing. I beg you, listen! Love is eternal, too, but you seem to have forgotten. I've begged you not to do this, not to leave my side. The sins of our enemies are in the past. Can you not let the memory of our losses rest?*

No, mother. I'll travel the universe in Kyllikki *in pursuit of my quest. After this is done, I'll come back to be with you. Until you die of old age. Until my brain is worn into nothing, my body an empty shell.*

I cannot condone this fool's errand, my son, and I cannot help you. But my love for you, being eternal, is such that I cannot stand in your way. I wash my hands of this.

Goodbye, then, mother. Godspeed. Perhaps we'll never meet again.

Bones, nerves, muscles, sinews, skin.

This might work, the scientist thought. *It must work.*

With a quick shiver, *Kyllikki* recovered the last splinters of the scientist's son. His skull, made of reinforced glass, shattered. The cavity empty, its content vaporized, worn into nothing.

The scientist raised her eyes and gazed out the panoramic window.

There is no Artificial Star R-15, she thought. *Louhi lied.*

The scientist noticed a shift in the three-dimensional map.

Kyllikki had consumed its sun's substance. With its hydrogen depleted, the star had become a red giant, devouring all that remained of Farmind and Saari—including the clear pool of algae in the deserted hospital's slanted floorboards.

Maybe I should have sent the Deactivation Key to Louhi after all, the scientist thought.

Kyllikki dived steadily into Tuonela's accretion disk.

The scientist could feel the event horizon approaching, the lengthened seconds' relentless pull. For the last time, she looked down at the empty shell that once contained her son.

She thought of his words again, and, finally, of his name:

I want to be eternal, mother.

I don't want to be eternal. Can't we go back to the normal family we were?

Go back, mother? What are you talking about? There is no way back.

There is! If you're willing to hold my hand again and follow me, just like when you were little. Because you are little now, Lemminkäinen. You've just been born a second time.

I can't take your hand anymore, nor will I follow.

Lemminkäinen!

I will see you at our only end, mother.

The scientist took her son's lifeless body in her arms and wept.

Action

INTO THE FIRE

I met Elya when she saved me from the wreckage of my overturned SUV at about four in the morning. She flipped the car upright before I'd taken any serious damage, aside from wounded pride. Dazed as she helped me out the passenger-side door, all I'd been able to ask her was how the hell she'd done that in the middle of the freezing desert night.

Elya told me, cheerfully, that she'd also crashed just a short way off. What were the chances? She didn't look like anything out of the ordinary just a petite, dark-skinned woman in drab, loose clothing whose eyes…well, all right. Her eyes. They glowed in the dark.

I asked her what she'd meant by that, *also crashed*, unable to look away from the eerie reddish light in her gaze as she checked me over in concern. Once she was sure I could stay on my feet and walk, she grabbed my hand like we'd known each other forever and led me a hundred sandy, cactus-ridden yards under the full moon. She pointed.

Earth's first honest-to-God openly extraterrestrial being had crashed here in what looked like one of our own spacecraft. What were the chances indeed?

Elya said her people had learned the design of such vessels from the wreckage of ours floating out in space. She'd always known surviving the landing was highly improbable, let alone ever returning home. I asked where that was, and no matter how many times she said it, I couldn't retain the information. Even *Elya* was as close as we could think to render her name in English while I drove her north to San Francisco in a sub-par rental.

Patiently, Elya explained that she'd been learning our language from broadcasts. She'd spent years deciphering everything about us with an eye toward practical contact, whereas academics on her world had only ever bothered with abstract knowledge and built replicas of our spacecraft. She said she'd come here as humanitarian aid, that it'd be a life well spent.

When I asked her what she meant by humanitarian aid, she said, "You have mythologies about superhumans. Superheroes. Just those tales give you so much hope. I'm like enough of them that I believe I can do what they do. I've pitied your kind for as long as I've admired you."

"You came here," I said, about ten hours and zero sleep later, "to save our sorry asses?"

Elya laughed. "Not from yourselves. Not from the wars you so foolishly start, either. But from accidents, disasters, recklessness…? Having saved *you*, I hit the ground running."

Elya's command of English was so precise that she'd even absorbed figures of speech and complex idioms. I was impressed by her immediate sense of humor, too—her affability, her seeming lack of regret at being stranded here. Sure, I'd been in medical admin for most of my fifteen years since college, but I'd studied enough linguistics and psychology to be impressed.

I told Elya she could crash with me for as long as she needed. That made her laugh, given the parallel ordeals that had brought us together. My apartment wasn't great, not the kind of place you'd want to cram two grown women—or at least two grown woman-shaped sentient beings—but the office was easy enough to convert back into a spare bedroom.

Rather than go out the next day to start applying for jobs, Elya went straight to the local authorities and asked them to call a press conference. They looked at her like she had two heads, which was a blatantly absurd expectation even for non-Earth creatures, until she proceeded to demonstrate the precise extent to which she couldn't be burnt, crushed, poisoned, or even bled out. She could heal instantaneously; her strength was at least three times that of an average human. Every medical test to which Elya voluntarily subjected herself verified more of the same. The media made a lot of comparisons to *X-Men* and similar comics, and not without cause. Flying without technology was about the only thing she couldn't do.

For better or worse, I became a sort of living switchboard for the reporters, podcasters, and concerned citizens who reached out. It helped that, in the process of shuttling Elya through the perpetual whirl of public scrutiny, I became a sort of friend. Living with someone, working with someone, *existing* with someone without exactly becoming friends?

Easily done, but not with Elya. She wasn't just genuinely likeable, but genuinely selfless. Anything you wanted to know, she'd tell without reservations. When all was said and done, no good came of it—not for all her genuinely altruistic intentions.

I was hesitant to participate in her interviews in those early days. I saw myself as more of a coordinator, a facilitator, a guide. Still, it was only a few months before Elya suggested I ought to give my account of how we'd met. So I did. Within another few months, I was able to give up my job and focus on the agency. Our operation didn't merit agency-with-a-capital-A, but that's what we called it jokingly. Elya understood both the humor and the irony.

It started small, the things people requested. Safeguarding of their kid on a first date, trailing behind like private investigators; patrolling neighborhoods at night to crack down on violent crime; that sort of thing. Saving people from fires, accidental or arson, happened a great deal during her time with us. There was also a building collapse on account of a series of earthquake tremors. She grew particularly adept at navigating rubble.

There were arrests. There were daring rescues. There were attempts on Elya's life, but none of the would-be assassins or clearly staged accidents succeeded.

Elya didn't accept payment for any of it, but donations toward operations came in. We kept a roof over our heads and a dedicated phone line open. The police department and city fire brigade brought her in on difficult missions and daring rescues. She was tireless, nearly bulletproof, and impervious to flame. They collaborated with her, sent her only into situations where mere mortal officers and volunteers would have been in genuine peril.

Where Elya called herself a team player, I called her reckless to the point of utter stupidity. And I did love her for it. How could I not love someone who'd saved so many lives?

After about a year, other state governments started asking questions. Why did California have a monopoly on Elya's heroics? Couldn't she tour? In the very least, Washington, D.C., strongly suggested she might spread her humanitarian efforts.

Abashed, Elya could only agree, so we packed up and went wherever there seemed to be greatest need. From forest fires in the Midwest to Gulf Coast flooding, she made as much of an impact as she could on monthlong stints in diverse locations. There was a lone close call that observers found shocking—Elya choking on smoke was cause for concern, especially to me.

"That's why you need to wear the masks when they're offered," I told her as she lay recovering, passing the crossword puzzle back. "Martyr isn't in the job description."

"It's not a job, Jess," Elya insisted, completing another word. "It's a calling."

Demand for Elya's presence made her more popular than any number of top performers. She went on talk shows in the US and abroad, but she refused to advertise for anything.

Nobody tried to assign her a superhero name, either. That was the wildest part of all, aside from the perpetual travel and lack of sleep. She wasn't Wonder Woman or Superlady or anything of the sort. Not even her signature glowing eyes played into it, because, as far as she knew, the glow did nothing to contribute to her abilities and immunities.

Elya was just Elya, no matter what news outlet you followed, no matter what language.

Once, I asked her if she was disappointed. She looked at me like she had that night in the desert, like I was adorable. That was the closest her pity ever came to touching me.

"Why should I want to be called anything other than my name?" Elya asked. "Your mythologies have meaning, and names have power. My name has earned its keep."

There was a disturbing trend on the rise near the middle of that fifth year. Local vigilance surrounding accidents of various kinds wasn't what it used to be, not given how single-handedly she'd helped the city. In a handful of instances where we hadn't made it to accident and crime scenes in time, serious injuries, even fatalities, were almost guaranteed.

Elya said she wished she had the ability to be in several places at once, or in the very least clone herself. Her sense of humor now had a darkness to it, and her laughter was no longer as light as I remembered it. I wouldn't have blamed her for second-guessing her self-assigned mission.

I suggested that Elya ramp up the PR dimension of her crusade to assist humanity by working with government safety officers nationwide to produce videos sort of like the ones you still saw on commercial flights. She agreed, but her charisma wasn't what it had been.

Why aren't more of Elya's kind on the way? one critic wrote. *Surely they understood the wealth and fame that would be theirs on arrival in a world like this. Why send only one?*

On reading the column in which those lines appeared, Elya withdrew from the media to focus more diligently on local, grassroots heroism. San Francisco hadn't seen much of her in the past several months; she'd come to think of herself as being from where I was from.

I begged her to take a month off before diving back into the local fray, as we hadn't had much time to ourselves. We'd become everything to each other, but we didn't wear that fact on our sleeves, or even flaunt it. In the public eye, I lived to serve Elya, and Elya lived to serve.

Elya relented, but said she'd only rest for a fortnight. That was better than nothing. We got caught up on the much-neglected press clippings book. We sorted digital photos and printed ones we wanted to put on the bulletin boards and fridge. We'd never really grown past being scrappy roommates, scrappy friends, and even scrappier lovers.

We'd met because we crashed our respective vehicles, after all. There were no photographs to commemorate that night in the Sonoran Desert, but I wouldn't forget the way the sunrise looked just beyond her as we walked out of the sand and into civilization. A sky on fire, and Elya right in the thick of it. I had never believed in foreshadowing outside the realms of literature and other forms of fiction, but I should have.

San Francisco had been overdue for not just an earthquake, but also a major blaze. It shouldn't have shocked either of us that a fire cut our brief holiday to the quick, sent Elya rushing barefoot into the night as I chased her with boots and the industrial smoke mask I'd bought her. She vanished into the chaos before I could get her into either one.

Elya had assisted in dozens of smaller local fires, none of which had proved close calls like that forest fire in the Midwest. Sheer luck of the draw. She'd been good at retrieving people from wreckage at minimal risk to herself. The smoke incident had been a one-off; she'd taken to covering her face thereafter.

It's estimated that Elya assisted local authorities in the rescues of at least a hundred people that night before vanishing into an office complex that collapsed seconds later.

Digging her way out of rubble, healing—that should have been easy. The entire building was up in flames, though, and she hadn't let me catch up to give her the mask.

Elya's death by smoke inhalation—suffocation—was hailed as a national tragedy.

Everyone mourned as if they'd lost a beloved political leader, as befitted the world's first nonhuman resident *and* superhero. I didn't let my personal grief enter into the equation, refused to accept recognition beyond what I'd always received as her assistant and companion.

The fallout from Elya's crusade, now at an end, became much more obvious than the scattered handful of incidents with elevated fatalities the city had already seen. In the eight months following her death, more fires started on account of carelessly pitched cigarettes in both urban and rural areas. People didn't wear seat belts as scrupulously as they once had, either, on account of her swift assistance at the scenes of crashes like mine.

For every effort state and local governments made to convene committees on preparedness, there were a dozen public protests. People wanted to blame someone for Elya's loss. Simultaneously, they were also asking how we had grown so complacent due to the rescue efforts of one alien creature.

About a year after the funeral, which had been attended by hundreds locally and thousands by broadcast, I made a solitary trip south to where—for me, at least, and for her above all—it had started. I made the drive with a kind of recklessness that might've resulted in another crash had it not been daylight.

There was nothing to mark the spot where I'd crashed, and nothing to mark the spot where she'd landed, either. We'd always been cagey about that, always wanted one secret that was ours and *only* ours. I remembered the scattering of cacti, the way it had framed where she landed. The wreckage of her craft had gone to the Smithsonian, and replicas in scores of museums worldwide. The positive impact she'd made in under a decade was extraordinary—as was the negative, but nobody was discussing it in those terms, not yet.

We'd forgotten, to a degree, how to be self-reliant. How to save ourselves from dangers to which we'd spent centuries perfecting our responses. Thousands of years, even, if you thought back to antiquity. No disaster would be unique, be a miracle anymore thanks to Elya's intervention. What Elya had truly offered, beyond her powers, was a kind of hope we didn't know how to locate within ourselves—being mere, insecure mortals.

On the spot where Elya crashed, or as close as I could manage, I left the mask.

NOT SO DIFFERENT

Have you turned the mic on? Ah, splendid. Thank you.

According to the warden, you're here today to let me talk. No questions to lead me on, that was my only stipulation. Get it all out there, as it were, my side of the story on this whole Gifted business. But are you sure I'm the voice for the job?

Guess that nod means yes. Maybe I can understand why you don't want to talk directly to *her*, especially given what she can do. Heaven knows it's what landed me here, although—it landed her here, too. Taking me out was pride before the fall.

Melinda Lim was no ordinary child, I can tell you that much.

We were classmates from elementary school on, and we even ran in some of the same circles at university. She was quiet at first, how's that for irony? Almost never spoke. When she did, though, you couldn't help but listen. It's like the rest of the world would just...fall away. Even a noisy playground was no match for Mel. And if what that riveting voice was saying contained some kind of request, or a command, or even a mere suggestion—*Wouldn't it be nice if you picked me that clover, Finn?*—you'd do it. Just like that.

Mel could've done unspeakable things. Children possess the capacity for astonishing cruelty, to such a degree that none of the other Gifted currently known to the world could have stopped her even then. But all she did when we were young was ask for innocuous things—flowers, help with homework, my presence beside her at lunch.

Mel wasn't a popular child, and she wasn't a popular teenager, either. By then, most of our peers had gotten the sense something was off. They steered clear.

I was the only person Mel told. We were in seventh grade when she pulled me aside and asked, "Why do you stay?"

"What, with you?" I remember asking. "We're friends, Mel. That's all there is to it. Mel and Finn forever, right?"

"I have a secret," Mel said quietly. "I think you know it. Thank you for never...resisting when I forget myself and..."

"I don't think it's possible to resist," I told her. "As Gifts go, Compulsion isn't that common, right? And you don't...*do things* with it."

"There are only three others out there," Mel said, "that we know about, anyway. Two of them are dead. They went...*yeah*. They turned."

"The living one's a government official or something in Australia, right? With a ton of regulations in place?"

Mel nodded, running her fingers through her hair. "And me. School admins and teachers know. The counselors, too."

"*And* me," I pointed out—to reassure her, you understand. "I won't give up your secret, Mel. I won't betray you."

The thing about Mel was, she'd internalized her parents' desire for her to live a normal life. They didn't want her getting mixed up in those grand, dangerous heroics you see the other Gifted engage in. Because Mel's gift wasn't anything to do with Flight or Telekinesis or Strength, any of that flashier stuff that got revered up until a few decades ago, they hoped she'd blend in. She really hoped that she would, too—and if she ever *did* use her Compulsion intentionally, it would be for good.

It's a no-brainer, of course, that she ended up in journalism. Somewhere along the line during college, no longer a naïve child, she decided she wanted it both ways. Wanted to use her Gift for good *and* blend in with the rest of us. Lead a perfectly normal life at home; pass off her knack for getting people to say and do exactly as instructed as uncanny investigative and reporting skills. She couldn't have devised a better method of cover.

Meanwhile, I was studying economics. We lost track of each other after undergrad; she went on to do an MA in Media Studies, and I opted for an MBA in Corporate Management. We both stayed in the city, of course. We loved our home.

When I say we lost track of each other, I mean we didn't communicate aside from cards exchanged on major holidays. Maybe the occasional social-media private message, just to check in on each other. We were both only children born to middle-class families; by the end of graduate school, our parents were all dead.

I can see you're dying to ask me *how*. You must pay attention to the news.

When my once-humble tech startup went public as a corporation, there was a gala. It was well covered by the media, well attended by invitees. I invited colleagues and competitors alike.]

Yes, friends and family as well. Should I even tell you what comes next? You already know.

Peculiar that the attack should have come during the after-party. Even more curious that it was while Mel and I were catching up at the VIP-lounge bar for the first time in five years.

Her parents died in the blast, out in the theater lobby—and so did mine. Along with a significant number of my then competitors, mind, whose companies taking hits did *nothing* for healthy competition. I'm a free-market advocate, a staunch capitalist. Tragic.

"I don't understand, Finn," sobbed Mel, as I did my best to hold her back while the paramedics and law enforcement officers did their job. "Your security's second to none."

"There are those who'd stop at nothing to see me fail," I said quietly, stroking her hair.

"Who'd see you suffer, too?" Mel asked, sniffling all over my lapel. "And personally?"

I shrugged, wrangling my handkerchief out of my pocket. "Do saboteurs possess reason?"

Mel blew her nose and rested her head against my shoulder. "Do *you* think that they do?"

She could have used her Gift on me at that time, but she didn't. Always incredibly trusting.

Over the back half of that decade, in spite of my competitors' losses, Trevelyan Technologies emerged as a prime innovator on the world stage. I didn't stop at computing, didn't stop at security and monitoring, didn't even stop at transportation.

There were the inevitable scandals, the inevitable investigations into my business practices once my competitors recovered. None of their inquiries turned up anything. Why would they? The public trusted my brand implicitly. They had every reason to do so.

We rebranded as TrevTech about the time Mel launched *her* first investigation, which was twelve years after the blast. There was another gala, this time uneventful.

Mel had gone on to become a jack of all journalistic trades—major written features printed in almost every major world paper, occasional front-line anchor reporting from protests and war zones, you name it. Everything but the kitchen sink, just shy of a Pulitzer.

Melinda Lim could get the truth, no matter the cost. People said her fearlessness came of losing everything. I still believe that, even if her rising pride was also to blame.

The thing was, people had begun to *notice* how good she was. They didn't understand how earnest questioning could yield results, even with the wiliest politicians.

The last presidential administration investigated *her*. You probably remember that, too. While Washington found nothing on her—nothing they were willing to take public, out of *decency*, the spokesperson said—she found nothing on me. Nothing *she* was willing to take public.

World media outlets and governments were distracted at the time, of course. Incidents involving rogue Gifted were on the rise. Turned, that was how Mel always put it. Gifted who *turned*.

If you had, say, Flight or Strength or Telekinesis and decided to use it for the public good, that was vigilantism. If you had Mindreading and used it for personal gain, that was a felony.

The law tolerated such things for a while, of course. We all did. In those early years of cracking down, it was mostly the flashy ones who got caught and put away. Prisons like this one, mental institutions—the punishment did tend to fit the crime. Physical Gift infractions were most likely to serve time, whereas Psychological Gifts, *if* you got caught? Meant being committed.

Mel called me the week after TrevTech went global. That must have been at about the fifteen-year point. There weren't many Gifted left out there, at least not ones living openly.

After terse congratulations, she said, "I still think you might be up to something, know that?"

"Thank you," I replied. "I still think *you* might be up to something, too. Checkmate much?"

Mel made a frustrated noise on the end of the line. "That's how it's been for a while now."

"What they did to Prime Minister Eccles, way Down Under—unfortunate, wasn't it?"

"He wasn't using his Gift," Mel said, toneless and cautious. "He never did. I could always tell."

"It would be a shame if someone ever found out about you," I said, and maybe even meant it.

"Eccles, his mistake..." Mel's voice hardened. "Was registering himself in the first place."

"Quite a lot of you thought that was smart," I reminded her. "The way forward, even. Safer."

"My parents didn't," Mel shot back. "They wouldn't hear of it. Always protecting me."

"Yes," I agreed, "and you went on to protect yourself. You could've done what Eccles did."

Mel was quiet for long, long seconds before she said, "You're protecting yourself, too, Finn."

I can't remember how the rest of that conversation went. Maybe she hung up on me; maybe I hung up on her. Our fondness for each other had worn so thin I could no longer feel it.

You've been extremely patient with me in spite of these personal digressions. But the personal's bound up in the public record; you're smart enough to recognize that. You're smart enough to keep your mouth shut, too, lest you fall under suspicion.

Besides, giving an inmate like me—a lifer—enough rope to hang himself is economical. I can appreciate that. Someone told me you're writing a book on this sordid affair. Fair exchange, no robbery. I'll live in infamy, isn't that how they say it? *Do* they still say it?

It's been a long time. Longer than a bright young thing like you has been living.

How far had I led us down this lamentable memory lane? Ah, indeed. Thank you for the finger-count; I appreciate it. The fifteen-to-twenty-year stretch is where it gets *good*.

Mel spent those last five years of freedom dialing her pride up to eleven. She took out a number of the politicians behind crackdowns on the Gifted. She took out a number of businessfolk like me, too. She took up photography, which hadn't been in her initial skill set—and, you guessed it, got shots so improbable *that* was what tipped public favor away from her.

Meanwhile, Mel had been exhaustively researching the gala blast. She'd always been a tenacious one, had never known when to let sleeping cinders lie. Her mistake wasn't so much researching events surrounding the blast; it was flat-out researching *me*.

One night almost twenty-one years to the day—approaching the blast's anniversary, of course—she got to my new security detail. All however-many dozen of them. Hard to recall. All she needed was to Compel external security to buzz her in and go home once they had.

All she needed once she was inside was to work her way floor by floor—asking my team to show her anything she liked, taking photographs as she went. Asking them for copies of data in whatever formats struck her fancy. I think she went for memory sticks and disks to make the insult more personal. Those were what we grew up using.

There was nothing amiss for about forty-eight hours thereafter. She Compelled them all to cover the fact she'd ever been there. I would've been blissfully ignorant until the data went public, until she broke her story in whatever medium she'd see fit.

But I got a call the night before the gala blast's anniversary. This is where her pride comes in, and maybe mine, too. We could have come to an arrangement, spared ourselves indignity.

"I have it all," Mel said when I picked up, not even bothering with pleasantries. "Proof of what you've been doing—the buyouts, the money laundering, the cover-ups."

Now, I'd be lying if I didn't admit that I was terrified. I thought I could make her back down.

"Me and every other entrepreneur at my level, Mel. Do you think your dear public doesn't know that? Do you think they care? I make their smartphones, their VR devices. My transit infrastructure and jets get them from Point A to Point B. They're willing to look the other way for what I've let them afford. For *convenience*."

"You can't do this, Finn. You will not continue. And you'll tell them what you've done, tomorrow, before the world. You'll call a press conference. You'll tell them everything."

See, here's the conundrum—you can't *imitate* Compulsion. It simply exists, simply happens. We don't really know how any of the Gifts work, not for all my laboratories' attempts to crack it.

Mel forgot one crucial thing, though, in her emotion-driven grab for vengeance. Yes, the blast was mine. All of the other infractions she'd documented were mine, too.

That didn't much matter, not in light of the fact that *she* forgot to tell *me* to forget who'd commanded me to come clean. It was just part of the Compulsion, the knowledge she'd been the one to Compel me to call the press conference and confess.

So that's what I did. Live, on the air, on the anniversary of the blast. I told the world everything.

You've watched the footage, I imagine. It remains nearly viral to this day. You can stream it anywhere, call up the transcript in an instant.

But you can also call up the footage of the protests that followed in the days after they took me into custody. You can watch the outraged public demand Mel's head, too. They didn't just happen here at home. Australia took it up in solidarity, of course, after what happened with Eccles. Before the month was out, the marches and disruptions were worldwide.

If we can't rely on our beloved journalists to investigate and report honestly, who *can* we trust?

You look sad to hear all of this. Because you're a journalist, maybe—or because you're too young to remember what it initially meant for Gifted acceptance if they voluntarily registered with their national governments, or both?

On the first count, *I* trust you. Goes without saying. I wouldn't be talking to you otherwise.

The only mechanism through which any Gifted could find public acceptance to live openly *was*, in those days, to register. At lease people knew who they were and where they were. I'm not saying it's right—who am I to judge? Your job's to inform the public. These days, no Gifted can find acceptance anywhere, and not through registering, either.

It's why they hide now, like Mel did. It's why mob mentality forms when they're discovered.

There wasn't a trial for either one of us, which was a landmark occurrence at the time. By all previous procedure, I should've been the one to get a trial. Mel, not so much. None of the Gifted who'd been locked up and committed before her had been shown such mercy.

Criminals weren't being shown much, either, I can tell you want to point out. You have very expressive eyes. At least we know Compulsion requires all modes of human physical expression to work in conjunction. Those were the only findings of worth I ever uncovered.

Gifted or wrongdoer or *both*, what's the difference? Why show mercy to those of us who try to use our garden-variety exceptional talents for the greater good when you've already decided those who use their Gifts for the greater good don't deserve it?

Come the end of deliberations, Mel and I were both moved from detention to where you and I sit now. I say *prisoner*, but that's not necessarily what I am, what Mel is. We're not so different.

Quite a number of garden-variety greedy individuals would stop at nothing to succeed, but would they kill their parents? Their childhood best friend's? My motivations for killing my parents, Mel's, and several dozen other people—as well as my lack of remorse—were ruled insanity.

That phone conversation, the Compulsion, was the last time I ever spoke to Mel. I've seen her here on the inside. Always from a distance, always on transfers between wards.

You're a diligent gumshoe, so I'm sure you've researched what they do to people like Mel. What they do when it's a matter of expressiveness and persuasion, like it is with Mel. What they do when it's a matter of physical prowess. What they do when it's powers of the mind.

Talking to Mel would be useless, what when she lost her tongue. You could always request a written testimony for your book project, I guess.

Action

NO DEEPER THAN AN ESCAPE

Your earliest memory of water is the chlorine-bright tang of it filling your nostrils as you slip under, helpless to do anything except sink and stare up at the wavering fluorescent lights with wide, ripple-glazed eyes. You wonder if the instructor saw you go, if anyone saw you at all.

You've always liked the thought of creatures that lived underwater, always enjoyed feeding the fish in your grandfather's tank. You like helping him care for them, like making sure they'll live longer than the last ones and not make him sad.

And then, you wonder if you're really going to die. The thought doesn't hold, of course: a pair of strong arms hooks you by the armpits and drags you gasping back into the harsh glare of the land of the living. The air is heavy with humidity and chlorine gas, but you breathe it in great, hungry gulps all the same.

You did not expect to be given a second chance. You think now that you'll live not only to help your grandfather with his fish, but maybe get to study the ocean one day—water and everything that lives in it. Mermaids, even.

Still, you sob all the way home, wrapped in a damp beach towel in the back of your mother's car. You're only five, but you feel disconsolate. You know something's missing.

"Sweetie," your mother says, "stop crying. We'll go get ice cream."

"I don't want ice cream!" you shout, sniffling. "Mermaids don't eat it!"

"Mermaids swim better than you did in class today," your mother says.

In the weeks to come, you learn how to hold your breath. You learn how to open your eyes underwater not long after that, and you cling to the side of the pool as you search the shadow-dappled bottom of the shallow end for signs of fins and scales.

You've been given a second chance, and you're not going to mess it up.

* * *

Your earliest memory of swimming—for surely, somewhere in the ebb and flow of days, you learned—is in your great-aunt's pool, age nine, under your grandfather's watchful eye. You take little interest in the floating mattress or the massage jets that erupt along the walls of the shallow end. Braver now than you were four years ago, you take risks.

You're all about the deep end, goggles and lung-bursting retrieval games, colored rings with weights inside that spin with mesmerizing slowness to the smooth floor of the twelve-foot chasm. You dive with dizzying grace, your ears already ringing with the change of pressure.

Down here, everything is clear, serene blue shot through with sunlight. Quick as a fish, you fetch two rings, but that's not the reason you're down here. You haven't forgotten what you used to look for, whether adults insist it was something out of a fairy tale or not.

Down here, there are grotesque wonders such as you've never seen: balls of dead daddy longlegs that drift past like tumbleweeds, tiny drowned garden frogs flashing pale bellies as they drift. Once, you even found a butterfly, its wings stripped down to crystal translucency limned in remnants of black and orange.

These grotesqueries vanish, sometimes, what when you saw them only an hour before. You wonder if something is eating them. You've been told mermaids aren't real, but you can't think of an explanation, scientific or otherwise, for the vanishing dead things.

You finally break the surface, all ten rings in hand.

Your grandfather breathes a labored sigh of relief. You know that he's been ill, and that's why he has difficulty breathing. He's been like this for years.

"You didn't see those glasses Aunt Red lost, did you?"

You shake your head. "I saw dead spiders and frogs."

"I'll have a word with Red about cleaning the pool. You're too small to get it all out."

You've never seen any sign of mermaids living in the pool, but you're worried about them anyway. What if they scavenge for food, grateful for the spiders and frogs? This is why you don't clean the pool with the net, even when you're asked. You just pretend to.

"They're gross, but I don't mind that much," you say uncertainly.

You're waiting for your chance, so you keep diving—keep *looking*.

* * *

Your earliest memory of the ocean is bleak and beautiful, a family vacation gone awry because your parents weren't speaking to each other. You are twelve. Your first morning on the beach is a bleached, rainy expanse of white sand and grey sky.

While the others huddle beneath blankets and umbrellas, you trawl the clear, sand-swirled shallows for coquina clams, sand crabs, and starfish. You used to catch tadpoles, crayfish, and even snakes around the family campground's pond. You're not afraid. You're doing well in school, and you learned that marine biology is something you can study.

You also learned regular biology is something else you can study. Medicine, even.

Already knee-deep in the surf, you venture further out from the sandy shore.

The ghosts in the glassy water are many: slow, drifting shades dragged in and out again, relentlessly, without end. You find things more amazing than at the bottom of Red's pool.

Rubbery, dark green seaweed the size of a dead man's hand. Disembodied lobster claws. Tiny, quick larvae destined to die in tide pools. Twist ties from bags of bread. Soda bottles without messages. A butterfly, borne upon the swells by its splayed wings, legs thrashing.

It's the business of saving the butterfly that prevents you from venturing further. After all, it didn't *ask* to drown. At least you're fairly sure it didn't, what with how it thrashed.

You feel guilty you didn't leave it for the mermaids, but they have fish, too.

Later on, at the hotel, your father peers into your bucket and wrinkles his nose.

"Dump that stuff out. We can't take it on the drive home. It'll stink up the car."

Before you can explain that you'd like to take it back for the mermaids who aren't lucky enough to live in the ocean, you bite your tongue. You're just old enough to obey.

Carrying the bucket down to the beach at dusk might be dangerous. You don't know anyone in this state, and there are plenty of strangers. Still, the beach is quiet and cold.

Dumping your treasures back into the shallows, you watch the tide sweep them away. Shells, at least, your mother said you could keep. They're dry and pretty, and as long as you bleach them, they won't make the car smell on the ten-hour drive home.

You think of your grandfather and *his* fish, and of his ever-diminishing breath. You think about researching his illness one day, about finding a cure for him.

You stand there, motionless and melancholy, until the tide comes in.

* * *

Your next chance comes several years later, on another family vacation that goes only marginally better. It could be that you are fifteen, interested in fantasy novels and your studies at school, more isolated from the rest of your family than ever.

Or it could be that you're tired of listening, tired of being told that the worlds you dream are not only undesirable, but impossible. Science simply hasn't delved deep enough.

The evening sky is violent, a splintering of flame-hues as sunset erupts, a kind of prescient warning. You are swimming toward the horizon, which never gets any closer—in salt water up to your chin, jumping into each oncoming wave just as it crests.

The one that tows you under steals your breath.

You'd been planning this, true, but perhaps not so soon. Still, you feel a curious calm settle in your bones as you're tossed this way and that, eyes screwed shut, mouth clamped.

The time you're underwater feels infinite; your body feels weightless. You swear it flips you in a somersault, your curled body a pinwheel, your toes not even breaking the surface.

I'll never see daylight again, you think, a weird thrill. *I'm gone*.

You'll miss your youngest sister, and maybe a few friends from school. You'll miss your science teachers and the lab, the extra experiments they let you conduct.

You'll miss your grandfather most of all, knowing you won't get to help him.

Your breath's handed back to you as the wave slaps you brusquely to shore. Flat on your back, limbs flailing. Each breath sears in your lungs as the smoldering sun sinks lower.

Later, when you tell your little brother you almost drowned, he doesn't believe it.

"Liar," he says, breath whistling through the space where his front teeth fell out.

"How would you know," you mutter scornfully. "You can't even swim yet."

Your brother runs off crying to your parents. You're not allowed to swim for the remainder of the trip, which is the least fair sentence you can imagine.

Are the mermaids still hungry? Do *they* have answers?

Sometimes, you wish you hadn't saved that butterfly.

* * *

Subsequent chances are not so easily bought, and as the years pass, the water recedes from you, hesitant and elusive. There have been the odd trips to your great-aunt's pool, but those have largely been occupied with the task of teaching your younger siblings, a brother and several sisters, to swim. You try not to remember your near drowning as a thwarted adventure.

You no longer call on the poor, twisted spiders and frogs, and most of the colored rings have been lost or damaged. Cracked and deprived of the sand that once weighted them, they float, listless shells fading in the blistering sun. Your little sisters like to chew on them, and yanking them from angry toddlers' fists is less fun than fetching them from the depths.

Every once in a while, though, you steal away beneath the surface, welcoming the muted embrace like a lost lover. Your skin is stripped white in the watery dusk, glows periwinkle with shadows and the lingering promise of stopped, transformed lungs.

You don't feel human. You don't want to *be* human, not if it means dying the way that your grandfather is slowly wasting away. You've always thought of death as a door.

Your need for goggles is long past; you see clearly down here, open and unafraid.

The kick of your newest sister's fat baby legs and the swish of life preservers rob you of the illusion that this meeting between you and your beloved is in any way private.

You kick off from the wall, determined to spend the last few minutes with your fingers laced in your wayward, imagined siren's hair. Her fluid, rippling limbs pass over the planes of your body as you twist with an ecstatic shudder. Your breath hitches.

Seventeen now, you know that mermaids and sirens are different.

You break the surface, disoriented, greeted by your sister's childish squeals and your grandfather's panicked chiding. He's more frail than ever, breathing with a machine that they say will at least keep him alive until you finish college.

Your parents are too busy chatting to notice.

"You shouldn't hold your breath that long," says your grandfather, with a nervous grin.

"I'm practicing," you tell him, laughing it off. "I want to break the Guinness Record."

"That's totally dumb," your brother says from where he's drifting on a pool noodle.

Twelve feet down, the full moon's unstable reflection convulses.

Your siren's wan, nebulous sliver of a face is stricken with loss.

Treading chlorinated water, you have never felt more alone.

*   *   *

The next time you go under is not graceful. At twenty-two, you're set to graduate from college early, your biology major nearly complete. You've won awards for research papers, and you assist one of your professors on a project that might help people with your grandfather's illness. You want to help more than just your own flesh and blood.

Your hair has been dyed blue for months, faded to silvery glory by three months' harsh sun. You have a girlfriend. You are already applying for graduate programs.

The Blackwater River is motionless and inscrutable, save for the cut of your oars and the thick carpet of water lilies that breaks now and again to reveal a sinister tracery of stems and roots that vanishes down into the tarry, tannin-laced murk.

Your oar gets caught in them repeatedly. Each time you sever a blossom, you shiver.

Up ahead, one of your friends, who grew up around here, is telling the story of how a woman drowned one evening when she and her family were out paddling. Every time the police boats passed, she'd feared she might spot the body tangled amongst the lilies.

You think of what that woman, who they never did find, must have found beyond death's doorstep. You wonder if she feels more at home in the world beneath the murky ripples than she ever did in the sunlight, if the sirens swam this far inland to welcome her.

You're struck from behind by someone else's oar.

The world tilts, floods wet and dark. No loving siren's arms, these cold, raw stalks; no comforting blanket of blue, these blank, black ripples that stretch ever upward to the empty sky. You scrabble back into the boat: thrust forth from the current, unwelcome. You never even touched bottom, although you know it can't be more than five or six feet below.

No deeper than a grave, you think. *No deeper than an escape.*

Your friends comment on the appropriateness of your hair.

*   *   *

Your first memory of the Mediterranean is surreal, untainted: cerulean water ruffled by a light breeze, laced with tiny jellyfish. From your vantage point on the cruise ship balcony, they look almost like a painting come to life.

Twenty-nine now, you're someone's wife. You're also about to defend your doctoral thesis, having been supervised for the past several years by the professor whose project you've been working on. No one ever thought you'd get this close to a cure.

Contentment outside the lab has eluded you at every turn, although not for lack of trying. Your husband is not a gracious man anymore, although everyone else persists in thinking he is. Something is missing in your marriage, and something is missing in your research.

You step up onto the railing and curl your toes into the space between the metal bar and the thick glass barrier, longing. You wonder what it would feel like to dive in.

The jellyfish would cushion your landing, soft and yielding as a dream.

The water would close around you like silk, like the fine dressing gown you'd always wanted. The ship would pass over you, rocking you gently in its ponderous, unhurried wake.

Your husband—asleep in the cabin, with his cruel eyes and falsely kind face—would mourn. Everyone would believe him, which is a terrifying consideration. It gives you pause.

Your grandfather is in hospice care, and your parents are divorced.

Your brother wouldn't attend your funeral if it came down to it, because he doesn't approve of you any more now than he did when you were children. Your sisters, now teenagers, would be dragged along by your restrained, distant mother.

You, the only person who knows better—knows their hypocrisies—would be gone.

Your siren would come for you then, wrapping you close in smooth scales. You'd drift down to sleep in her arms, and wake to an underwater world everlasting.

You might even find what, in the realm of research, continues to elude you.

* * *

Several more years pass—and they are neither patient, nor kind. The sea's turmoil is closer than it has ever been, both outside and within, but you reach for it less and less.

Living on land has instigated other plans, ones you never would've foreseen. When you do walk the shore, it's for brief intervals only, picking your way carefully across perilous tide pools in search of glass. This coast is too cold for the baring of skin, the sharing of limbs.

Your husband doesn't even hide his cruelty now. While your body is safe from blows, it is seemingly safe from every other form of touch as well. Your mind and heart are another story, flayed by disparaging words and paranoid constraints.

Your colleagues at the pharmaceuticals company ask why you work such late hours, what when the treatment you've developed prolongs life for people with your grandfather's illness by a decade or more. Why you can't accept that your research has hit a dead end.

Your grandfather, alive in hospice thanks to the drug, seems sadder every time you see him. There's a question he wants to ask, but you hope he won't.

Your friends steal you away to the shore because they know it's the only thing that cheers you. They ask you if you're doing all right, their every word laden with concerned meaning.

"We could give you a place to stay," offers one of them. "My roommates won't mind. One of them has been through this, not too long ago."

You decide that's the best thing to do, agreeing that you'll pack up over the next few days and be ready Saturday morning. Abstractly, as you bend to investigate a pair of tiny, tussling hermit crabs, you wonder what it would be like to carry home on your back.

The sea aches where it touches your salt-parched hands, drawing your hands deeper into the tide pool's silt. The hermit crabs scatter, guiltily caught out. You thrust your hands as deep into the sandy muck as you can, feeling for shells. Maybe you'll find a home of your own.

Come back to me, pleads the siren. *I've grown cold.*

You shy from her fingers, leaping to the next rock.

You find a living starfish. A worn shard of delftware. Fossil shells. The kelp shreds of a promise you'd meant to keep, the disappointment of too many chances wasted.

I can't, you say. *I don't remember how to swim.*

Love, she replies, *you don't need his permission.*

It's then that your foot slips, just as the tide is coming back in.

Or you *tell* yourself that's what happens, smiling as you sink.

* * *

You're flat on your back again, breath knocked to nothing.

As the grey sky spins, turning your thoughts to sand, you feel warmth at the base of your skull and searing pain at the small of your back. The starfish slips free of your grasp, sinks soundlessly to the bottom. You know there's no going back.

You want to apologize to your grandfather for what you didn't find, that you didn't stay alive, not in *his* world, long enough to see how long he'll survive.

You read the signs, whispers the water as it rises, lapping at your ears. *You always knew.*

You try to nod. The warmth spreads, mingling with the water as it laps at your chin, glossing your parted lips with exquisite salt. The taste is everything that chlorine is not. It reminds you of what it meant to embrace the unknown, to pitch into that pinwheel dive.

Even the undertow is gentler than you remember, working for you instead of against. Maybe the first time, it was because you were too young—didn't yet understand living or loving, twin coins lifted from your eyes as just now you went under.

You have never belonged in any of the places you have attempted to exist, but the water has welcomed you at every turn. Landlocked or oceanic, it let you remain a little while, from time to time, even back when it couldn't let you stay.

Submerged now, you open your eyes. Your skin's stripped white again, limned in sunlight and shadow from the surface. There are no drowned, stagnant disappointments like you used to find in the deep end of Aunt Red's pool. The sea does right by its dead.

Swimming without hindrance, you find that, although your lungs have stilled within the hollow of your chest, you can breathe. Even your limbs feel lighter; even your heart still beats.

Above all things, that last hard-won victory means the most. You have survived with your heart intact against all odds. Nonetheless, your pulse stutters when you finally *see*—

Your siren arrives like the wayward lover she is, smiling with arms outstretched. She is clumsy-fingered with seaweed, but lovelier than the face of the moon. Her kiss chaste and hesitant. She has been more patient than you could possibly have deserved, but judgments like

I've missed you, you say with joy, and she surrounds you. *Kept trying to reach you.*

You didn't need anyone else's permission, says the siren. *You needed your own.*

One last breath, and your nostrils flood with the heady, sharp scent of her. Your ears fill with scuttling whispers, the promise of glass and shells beyond your wildest dreams.

Your siren will keep the cruel, dead men's hands at bay. She'll protect you from jealous, drowned women and those dull, indifferent water lilies set adrift on a poisoned river.

You'll whisper to her as you follow the tides to terra incognita: tide pools unexplored and creatures of the deep you've only dreamed. Your memories of a sunlit world become the siren's cautionary tales. She asks you if claiming your freedom was worth the fight.

Nodding, you welcome her with your eyes wide open.

All around is the cool, silvery blue of your faded hair.

How long do your kind live? Our kind? you ask, curious. *Will we live?*

For always, the siren says, kissing you on the mouth. *It's in our blood.*

* * *

There is some truth to the old stories about selkies, and it applies to sirens, too.

You can shed your skin. Your lover teaches you how, by night, and so you do.

When you return to work the graveyard shift in the lab, your colleagues are astonished. You've been missing for months, they tell you. Presumed dead.

Your family had even held a memorial not that long ago. You're touched.

You take the first vial of your own blood on the first night you're alone, your eyes widening at the pale, silvery blue of it. You describe it, analyze it, run test after test.

By day, beneath the waves, your lover asks why you've grown so tired, so thin.

The first time you go to your grandfather, explaining you've been authorized to oversee his care, his eyes narrow. He asks where you've been all this time, asks if those swimming lessons in Red's pool all those years ago have finally paid off.

"Yes," you tell him, and hand him your notes before you show him the vial.

After a while, he stops reading and stares. "I've lived too long already. *No*."

Fury gives way to sadness, but you still say, "I could administer it while you sleep. Think of how much it will help you. Think of how much it will help everyone *like* you. Even people suffering from other things. Even just—well, just *people*. Anyone."

"We were not meant to be deathless," your grandfather says, regretful.

You press the vial into his hands, kiss him on the forehead before you go, and beg him to reconsider. You tell him you'll come back once he's decided.

When the call comes one night in the lab as you work, hair still damp from your arrival on land, it is not what you expect. It is not what you expect.

Your grandfather, after weeks of refusing even standard treatment, is dead.

Your cure, in the hands of men who wish to speak with you, is anything *but*.

* * *

Within a decade's time, shedding your skin is no longer something you wish to do.

At first, you gave enthusiastic assent. Told the men into whose hands your vial had fallen that your only wish was for your cure to save lives. To extend them, even.

What became of your cure was something much more, something more sinister.

Those with your grandfather's illness—with any illness—were not the first to receive it. Your country's government administered it first to soldiers, claiming that to prevent casualties in battle was your cure's noblest use.

War could only last for so long in the world as it had become, wearying and unsustainable. Troops came home to their overjoyed families after the armistice.

Your country's government—and, soon, all the world's governments—said that there was no reason for death on *or* off the battlefield, not anymore.

Your lover did not appreciate her people's secret, now *your* people's secret, being shared. But she allowed that even immortal humans, at such a trace and artificially replicated dose, could not breathe underwater. Thank goodness for *that*.

Within a decade's time, overpopulation had already begun to skyrocket. War was no longer an answer, not since you had enabled them to conquer death.

Your country's government, all the world's, looked to *you* for an answer.

Unable to respond, you left, having shed your skin for the very last time. Your family will mourn your disappearance eternally this time, disconsolate.

Now, you're trapped, too—beneath the waves, no deeper than an escape.

In Action

LIKE WATER
MEETS WATER

In the river, trash and foam abound.

The cat tries to regain control of its limbs and swim to the surface, but its muscles will not comply. It is falling, confined, subdued by the torrents.

And yet, for the first time in centuries, it feels free again—as if in its original spirit-form, shapeless and intangible. Once, as the water deity it was, it had taken the form of a gentle mist in the depths of a mountain valley. It had frolicked through the wispy hair of a girl dressed in coarse linen, who stood beside a calm pond.

After leaving her offering of incense and prayers on the bank, she bent toward her reflection in the water and plaited her hair, with bits of wet earth beneath her fingernails. She had done as centuries upon centuries of her ancestors had done before her: left an offering and asked for health, safety, and prosperity. For protection from the ills ever encroaching upon their secluded world, which the cat, in its original guise, had always granted its devotees.

How the cat once wondered what a touch from those damp, sun-kissed fingers would have felt like! Curiosity or craving, it can no longer remember why it had begun to long for such things. Perhaps it had grown bored with century upon century of smoke drifting over the water of its lonely pond, of words that brought reverence, but no comfort.

Yes, it had grown tired of watching and granting what essentially amounted to wishes. The humans it had kept safe, protected, and seen grow invariably turned to each other for warmth and companionship. Incense and prayers offered honor, but they did not offer such enticing engagements as this.

The cat—the deity, the spirit, whatever it once was—can no longer think, caught in the rapids. Its fur is soaked by freezing water, and its nose coated in silt—like that mud-caked kitten, curled on the steaming curb, quivering in the heat after a summer downpour.

The cat was starving back then. Persistent hunger had diminished its pride. So, it stood beneath the awning of a butcher shop, and meowed and meowed. Hunger had been a hard thing to learn, and it had not known how to hunt, not yet, like a normal cat. The seasoning of the meat was piquant, its aroma sharp enough to make the cat's eyes water and its nose run. The scent forced it to stop crying and groom its face with its paws.

When the cat had first become a cat, it had not known how to groom itself, either. Its eyes crusted with tears, and its nose ran, causing dirt to stick to its eyelids and nostrils. But the cat saw the kitten and knew the mud would dry, and that the kitten would be too weak to clean it off.

The cat knew what suffocation was; it had protected humans from that, from what they called *drowning*, if they spent too long underwater in its former pond. Still, the cat reminded itself that it was not obliged to help. It had no obligation to any living creature—not to any cat, not to any human. It had kept generations of humans safe, and where had that led?

Humans! Such vain creatures, believing themselves above all other mortal beings on earth, showing so much terror at the prospect of death. What use had their offerings been? What use was fear in the face of the inevitable? The cat, the spirit, had protected them from danger in the short term, but death had always come for them in the end.

The cat has seen its providers perish so many times as to lose count. Centuries ago, humans held luxurious funerals drenched in perfume and incense. The cat hadn't been able to bear the smell, not after all those useless offerings, so it ran across the tile-paved roof and chased after the frightened spirit of the deceased. She was barely eighteen, the mother of four, and had once thrown a gilded porcelain cup at the wall. One of the flying shards had pierced the cat's eye and blinded it, but the cat received profuse, attentive care as a result.

The warmth and attention had been worth it in those early days as a cat, novel and miraculous. Human touch, for a time, had been everything it had hoped for.

On that incense-suffused day, the woman's spirit smelled like tangled silk floss, freshly steeped tea leaves, and newly hammered gold hairpins inlaid with gems. Had the cat even been able to smell spirits back then, or did its seeming memories lie? Maybe it had been thinking of the girl by the pool. The dead woman had looked very much like her.

Yes, of course it had. It had consumed countless spirits when it was no more than a nebulous mist—the spirits of evildoers and unfaithful who got lost and died in the mountains, beasts and humans alike. On reflection, the cat finds its past abilities as startling as recognizing a one-eyed farm dog in a strange city. The dog should have died decades ago.

The cat feels something sharp and cold tug at its neck amidst the swirl of relentless water.

The metal shard of a boy's baseball bat once lodged in the dog's brain. Or maybe it was the wooden hook, in lieu of a hand, belonging to an old veteran by the roadside with cataracts clouding his eyes. But is the source of the cat's pain truly sharp and cold? Perhaps it is blunt and hot instead, as hot as the farm dog's breath escaping its yellowing teeth.

"Hot? Was the dog's breath even hot?"

"Why, it must have been. He was so energetic, but somehow dead at the same time. I could not feel even a shred of delight in him as him dragged me to an abandoned lot and ate me."

"Was that even the same dog, the one that ate you?"

"He had the same star-shaped scar over his blind left eye."

"Was the dog really dead? Undoubtedly, irrevocably dead?"

"That morning, I stole a disemboweled fish from an old tin pickling basin. Someone had caught the fish, readied it for pickling, and left the basin on their balcony. Times were hard, and I had not seen a fish in ages. So I jumped from my tree onto the balcony, snatched the fish, and fled. It was too bony and scaly, but the taste was worth dying for. I was new there, and nobody paid me any mind. The villagers thought that the dog was guilty of my crime. He had stolen many times before, that poor, starving cur. They dragged him to a bamboo copse and clubbed him to death. I trailed behind them all the way. I saw everything."

"He saw me, too."

"I still had spirit-sensibility back then. So, I thought, great, finally something for me to have fun with! Not that people hadn't been dying. A great many had died that year in the famine. But those haggard spirits didn't have any power. What little they had stuck to their souls like wood splinters mixed with watery mud. However, that beaten dog's ghost was vengeful. Restless."

"Yes, so I had fun. I toyed with him until I got so bored I yawned three times in a row. Played with that angry gust of gore-caked grey fur until the sun half-sank beneath the hills."

Sharp and cold or blunt and hot, the cat cannot feel the object prodding its neck anymore. It feels stiff and flimsy now, frigid and stinging. The cat opens its tired eyes for a split-second and catches a glimpse of the timid sun, its light diminished by turbulent water.

It reminds the cat of the young man who dyed his hair pink and had five piercings in each ear, who once held the cat down in a bathtub filled to the brim. Through ripples and bubbles that escaped its lungs, the cat stared at the dazzling aura of the ceiling lamp as the man's fingers tightened around its neck. This was not like the warm touches it had come to love.

In the next instant, the young man pulled the cat from the tub and held it close to his emaciated chest. The cat could smell tap water soaking through the man's bleached shirt, could feel the soaked patch expanding down toward his abdomen, his groin. He lowered his head, buried his nose in the cat's fur, and sobbed. He was an art student and had a thick bundle of sketch papers covered in depictions of the cat. Usually, he smelled of graphite, oil paint, and turpentine, but some nights he smelled of sweat and steam as he limped into the apartment.

"Maomao!" he would call. "Come here, Maomao."

But the cat would stay in its favorite spot on the couch.

The man had been the one who decided to bring the cat home. The cat had no obligation to obey him, none, when for so long it had renounced its godly duties and taken no traditional offerings. The young man would turn on the light, pick up the cat, and kiss the cat's head. The cat took delight in the warmth of his lips but was irked by his cold nose.

"Hey, listen," the man said as he squatted down in front of the cat and pressed his face close, their noses almost touching. "You never come when I call, and it's breaking my heart. If you keep this up, you'll get no dinner tomorrow. If you don't give love, you won't get any back. It's that simple. Understand?" And then he broke into laughter, and the cat knew he was only being dramatic to amuse himself.

Humans! What fools they are. The cat continued to ignore the young man and continued to get food, even after the young man had stopped eating.

The cat feels like a piece of paper now—drifting with the rapids, waiting to dissolve. It has grown thin, too long without the kind of nourishment that had once sustained it. The cat feels as if its organs have been squeezed from its body, like when its last provider squeezed the last bit of toothpaste into her mouth as her family readied the truck.

"Did they have a dog? Was it barking?"

"I don't remember. The girl's family helped her climb into the truck. She didn't object. I was at the window, watching as they drove away. The girl was sitting at the very back, hugging her knees. I could have kept her safe, but that wasn't my concern anymore. Ready to tumble onto the dirt road, graze her skin, and let her hair mix with dust."

"But yes, they had a dog. A good-natured one who had six pups. One was a stillbirth, pink and hairless. It had a star-shaped birthmark over its left eye."

"The spirit of that farm dog has been following you for ages."

"The dog remains one-eyed. How? I was blind in one eye for a few years. I fell off a roof and broke my neck. When I got up again, that eye was not blind. What is that dog?"

"Why are you asking now?"

"That dog even knew my secret. He knew my secret, and I don't know how. After he drank my blood and ate my flesh in the abandoned lot, he pulled a tarp over my remains and waited for me to reset in the darkness. So that he could eat me over and over."

"Was his breath hot or cold?"

"I don't know. Hot and blunt or cold and sharp? I don't know. It's like saying space and time or time and space. Does it matter? It lasted several days. For several days, I was like Prometheus on his cliff. That damned eagle! But I was no Prometheus. I thought maybe after resetting enough times, this body would not be able to feel pain anymore. That never came to be. Why did the dog know? Why did he do it? Why was he there? Why?"

"Consider it your punishment."

"My punishment. My—who are you? Why are you talking to me?"

"I am you. And I am speaking to you because we wish to be judged."

Suddenly, the world feels flat and still. Everything has fallen away—space and time, *and* time and space. For a moment, the cat thinks it has gone back to the attic bedroom of its last provider: empty, quiet, locked from the outside. Millions of dust motes float in the sunrays.

The cat lies in a patch of sun and looks at a branch out the window, its view confined by the window's four corners. It senses motion in this picturesque view, something tense and alert in a realm of slumbering heat.

The cat narrows its eyes and sees *itself* perched on the branch, sees itself struggling to peer through the window. It sees its own eyes, immense and round, its pupils thin slits. The cat has seen a lot through those eyes as it perched on a branch and peered through a window.

It once saw a sixteen-year-old call girl helping an elderly customer with his daily diabetes shot once her main job was through. That was the kind of warmth, the kind of connection, it had longed for. Once, in exchange for offerings, it might have done more than just protect the man—might even have healed him, had he been pious enough.

It once saw the profile of its pink-haired provider, lying on a blue-sheeted hospital bed with closed eyes and bloodless lips, as a nurse plunged a needle in his arm. It could have kept him safe, too, but it had been under no obligation.

The cat also saw its last provider fiddling with a needle in her shaky hands. Her skin was darker, and her blood vessels did not bulge like the others'—at least not at first. She tapped her forearm to relax the muscles.

The cat feels tired. What about those damp, sun-kissed fingers in a misty mountain valley by a pond? Where had they gone? The cat had once enjoyed watching those fingers light incense, folded in prayer, but now the only ones it can get are shaky and covered in sweat.

The cat is exhausted now, undone. It relaxes every last one of its muscles, allowing the water to flow into its senses and carry it away.

"Do you see your mistakes?"

"What mistakes?"

"The ones for which you are being punished."

"I didn't steal any fire. Didn't give humans anything they're not supposed to have. I only protected them when they prayed and made offerings to me."

"You are no Prometheus! Just a nameless trickster without a single worshipper left."

"Exactly. I have no power anymore, not for centuries, so what could I have done?"

"Think about the juvenile delinquent who used his metal baseball bat on that dog just to save you. Think about that call girl, who fed you sausages. Think about your pink-haired art

student, and so many more. Think of their deaths. What did you do when they died?"

"Huh," snorted the boy, as he picked the cat up by its scruff. His bat, tarnished by the dog's blood, gleamed in the afternoon sun. The boy grew to enjoy carrying the cat around on his broad shoulders as he roamed the streets, despite the teasing he got from fellow gangsters.

"Hi, sweetie," said the call girl, into the phone, finally reaching out for her own sake, "are you free this weekend? I'm thinking, it would be nice if we went somewhere together. What about that new café next to campus? Or the mall? Your outfits are all passé. I'll get you something nice. Hah, you're always so quick. Yes, I just got paid! A thousand just for one service! Isn't that great? What are you worried about? It's not like you can ask your parents for money. This is a necessary risk. Let's just have some fun, okay?"

"I'm going to die," said the young artist, who called the cat Maomao. His friend asked about his hospital stay, if it had done anything to help. "Only keeps me from dying this week," the artist said. "Won't cure me." His friend pleaded for him to go to another doctor, pleaded for him to live. "But why should I?" asked the artist, biting his lower lip.

The cat felt his tears dripping on its fur as it remained curled in his lap.

Why did he have to what? the cat wonders. *Have to live, or have to lie?*

The cat sinks to the river's bottom. Fine silt swirls between its paws. Junk litters the riverbed, some sharp as the blade of a fish knife and some blunt as the outline of a baseball bat. But all are cold, *so* cold—as cold as death, if death has a temperature. Water does, though, and water is often cold. The cat, the spirit, had grown tired of the cold, hadn't it?

What did I do when they died? The cat examines its memories, but finds nothing. *Time and space, space and time.* Memories litter its consciousness like junk litters the riverbed. *Where have they all gone?* the cat wonders, experiencing only misty lightheartedness.

"It's weird how my paintings are getting more cheerful," the art student said to himself, as he stood before his almost-completed painting of Prometheus.

The cat turned around. Unlike the bitter, agonized Prometheus on textbook covers, the art student's Prometheus had relaxed brows and closed eyes. There were no chains, no eagle to be found. The demigod extended his arms, as if embracing the pale-blue mountain in the distance. The artist smiled bitterly as he massaged his right arm. He left the room, and then returned with a fountain pen and bottle of ink. He used the pen to splatter Prometheus's chest with a fine, black spray of ink: a glaring blemish.

The cat finally went to the mud-caked kitten and moistened the clots on her eyes and nose with its tongue. It found a star-shaped birthmark over her left eye.

Oh no, the cat thought. It fled, leaving the kitten in the grip of summer heat.

It ran to the river, where its last provider—a little girl back then—was washing her hands.

She stretched her palm toward the cat, and it stood still. She giggled, ruffling its fur.

"You're not afraid of me," she said, her eyes amber-clear under the sunlight.

The cat closed its eyes to take in her caress—those damp, sun-kissed fingers.

How had they grown so cold, as cold as death? it wondered.

"It's that guy who drives a dirty minivan," whispered the old veteran who always sat on his bench by the dirt road, outside the village. "That guy sells evil spirits, I tell you. Stores evil spirits in that van of his." He kept his eyes fixed on the cat. "Please help us. You used to help us, back when my parents and their parents, and *their* parents before honored you. I still honor you. Please cleanse our corrupted youth. You are the only one who can help."

The cat gazed into the old man's cataract-covered eyes with suspicion, wondering whether he was a prophet or lunatic. Either way, the cat had no obligation to help, not anymore—not even the few humans who still left offerings at the pond in the mountains.

The cat's last provider grew into a woman with dead eyes, with needle tracks in her arms and bite marks on her hands. The cat could have kept her safe, it *could* have.

"Steal, I let you steal!" her father shouted, grabbing her by the arm, reaching for a bamboo pole in the corner of the room. The skin of the pole was worn with years of use.

For weeks, the provider buried her face in her hands or knees and mumbled only one thing. The cat could hear when it pressed its ears close.

"I don't wanna go to rehab. I don't wanna go to rehab. I don't wanna go to rehab."

On the morning of her departure, she finished the last of the powder she had hidden in her toothpaste tube and mounted the truck, her yellow dress swaying in the wind.

After the truck left, her sister realized that the cat was still in the attic and drove it away.

The cat wandered on its own for months, until it came across its last provider in a strange town at dusk. She was still in that yellow dress, being dragged out of a soiled grey building by a thin man in an open white coat—along with several other women.

They scattered into the street and talked to passing men, bargaining with them.

The cat followed its last provider to a motel. She led a drunken man inside and emerged alone hours later, clutching wrinkled money in one hand. She collapsed at the side of the road.

The cat rushed close, listening to the last of her breathy mumbling.

I don't wanna go to rehab. I don't wanna go to rehab. I don't...

The cat could smell her soul dissipating. Scent of fresh river water, dissipating.

The cat wandered off, unnerved. It longed to return to its carefree, wandering mood before it had seen her. Before long, it came to the leveed river, which emptied into the sea.

It could not tear its attention away from the beckoning, mesmeric rush of water.

The cat did not know why the sight of its last provider had affected it so deeply.

Maybe she was a symbol—a microcosm, the process of warm fingers turning cold. The girl by the pond, leaving offerings centuries upon centuries ago; the girl washing her hands in the leveed river. Both had loved cat, the spirit, in their way, hadn't they?

Maybe she represented an accumulation of too much failure and disappointment.

Or maybe the cat shouldn't be looking for any meaning at all.

It wondered what death would feel like, the same way it had wondered, centuries upon centuries ago, what human touch would feel like. What human *emotion* would feel like.

The cat stretched, setting its paws on the levee's edge. The action reminded the cat of the time it climbed onto the edge of the pink-haired art student's bathtub.

"Hi, Maomao," he said, lying down in the warm water, "thought you were afraid."

The cat observed the parts of him that were above the water. His knees were smooth, but one side of his chest was covered in purplish black spots like his blemished Prometheus.

The cat—the spirit, whichever—could have kept him safe. Could have healed him.

"Today I tried to lie, but that doctor saw through me," he said, "so I was refused again." He bit his lip. "I wonder why," he continued, "they all refuse me. I thought…that illness and death would bring us together. I believed suffering would make us one, like water meets water." He turned to the cat, burying his nose in its fur—somber and earnest, for the last time.

The cat opened its eyes wide, staring into the heartless, turbulent current. Food, touch, warmth, shelter. These things, too, had been offerings and reverence. It *had* failed.

Let's see if he was right, the cat thinks. *Let's see if I meet them there.*